"A blind date?"

Kristi laughed. "Yester[day] [at my]
aunt's Fourth of July ba[rbecue she wanted me to meet]
this guy who used to live across the street when I was
in high school."

"How did you handle it?"

"I told her I'd just met someone, and your name kind
of slipped out."

Nate's eyes narowed. "What is it with families?"

"They mean well," she said. "At least mine does. My
mom was a single parent, too, and it was hard for her."

"My family wants to find a new mother for Molly and
Martha." His voice was thick with resentment. "They
seem to think I'm in over my head."

"Oh, I'm sure they don't. Your girls are great. They're
happy. Anyone can see they're well cared for."

"So, how about it? You come to my sister's birthday
party, I'll go to your family barbecue, and we'll call it
even."

Say no. "Sure," she said instead.

He offered his hand to seal the deal. "It's a date."

She shook it. "A fake date."

"Make that two fake dates." He smiled and her insides
turned to jelly.

Dear Reader,

I'm not sure why, but people are often surprised to learn that after I completed a bachelor of science degree (with honors, I'm proud to say) I went on to do graduate work in earth sciences. Yes, that makes me a bit of a nerd, so you probably won't be surprised to learn that my absolute favorite show on television right now is *The Big Bang Theory*.

I've always wanted to turn a science geek into a sexy hero, and I hope you'll agree that Nate McTavish is that hero. He's one of those supersmart guys who knows lots of obscure facts about all sorts of things, and it's really just the mundane details of day-to-day life—like keeping house and raising four-year-old twins on his own—that gets him a little flummoxed from time to time.

Enter Kristi Callahan, the interior decorator he's hired to stage his house before it goes on the real-estate market. She might not have a PhD, but she knows a thing or two about being a single parent, and Nate could sure use a good teacher.

The Daddy Project is Kristi's story and the second of three books set in the beautiful city of Seattle, centered on three women who run a real-estate business called Ready Set Sold. Readers have already met Samantha the carpenter in *The Christmas Secret*, and Claire's story will be up next. I do hope you enjoy all three! I love to hear from readers, and I hope you'll visit my website at www.leemckenzie.com.

Happy reading!

Lee McKenzie

The Daddy Project

LEE MCKENZIE

HARLEQUIN®

entertain, enrich, inspire™

Recycling programs
for this product may
not exist in your area.

ISBN-13: 978-0-373-75436-6

THE DADDY PROJECT

ABOUT THE AUTHOR

From the time she was ten years old and read *Anne of Green Gables* and *Little Women*, Lee McKenzie knew she wanted to be a writer, just like Anne and Jo. In the intervening years, she has written everything from advertising copy to an honors thesis in paleontology, but becoming a four-time Golden Heart finalist and a Harlequin author are among her proudest accomplishments. Lee and her artist/teacher husband live on an island along Canada's west coast, and she loves to spend time with two of her best friends—her grown-up children.

Books by Lee McKenzie
HARLEQUIN AMERICAN ROMANCE

1167—THE MAN FOR MAGGIE
1192—WITH THIS RING
1316—FIREFIGHTER DADDY
1340—THE WEDDING BARGAIN
1380—THE CHRISTMAS SECRET

For Mom and Dad, with love.

Acknowledgment

Thank you Geoff W. for an excellent idea.

Chapter One

Kristi Callahan rang the doorbell of her dream home. A sprawling 1960s rancher with two fireplaces, a breezeway separating the house from the two-car garage, and enough West Coast flair to appeal to potential buyers searching for their own dream home in one of Seattle's family-friendliest neighborhoods. And it was just her luck to be on the wrong side of the door.

This house was well beyond the reach of a single mom raising a teenage daughter on a single mom's income, but that didn't stop her imagination from playing with the idea of actually living in a house like this someday. And since she'd been hired to get this one staged for the real estate market, she would at least get to put her personal stamp on the place before returning to reality. Her modest two-bedroom town house was no dream home, but it was hers. Or it would be hers in twenty-three and a half years.

The other reality was that by the time she and her team at Ready Set Sold were finished here, this client would get top dollar, even in today's less-than-stellar market, putting this house even further out of her reach.

Speaking of clients, she had an appointment and she was only five minutes late. Okay, eight, but surely Mr. and Mrs. McTavish hadn't given up on her and gone out. There was a big silver-colored SUV and two pink plastic tricycles parked in the driveway but that didn't necessarily mean anyone was home.

She dug her phone out of the side pocket of her bag. No messages, no missed calls. Taking care not to get tripped up by a tattered teddy bear missing half its stuffing and three small yellow rubber boots strewn across the wide front step, she rang the bell again, and waited. A moment later her patience was rewarded with footsteps, lots of them. Two identical faces with earnest blue eyes and blond Cindy Brady pigtails appeared in the glass sidelight next to the door. One had her thumb in her mouth; the other's pigtails were oddly askew. No doubt these were the tricycle riders. And then they were dwarfed by a huge dog whose head appeared above theirs, a panting, drooling Saint Bernard.

"Is your mommy home?" Kristi asked, loud enough so they could hear.

Their pigtails shook from side to side.

The dog pressed its moist nose against the glass.

Hmm. The children stared at her but made no attempt to summon a grown-up. Surely they hadn't been left here on their own with only a dog to look out for them. A dog that let loose a strand of drool that now slithered down one of the blond pigtails.

Gross. Kristi quickly looked away and reached for the doorbell yet again, pulling her hand back when another set of footsteps, heavier ones, approached from the other side of the door.

The man who opened it was wearing faded blue jeans, a gray T-shirt with what appeared to be a complicated chemical equation in green lettering stretching across his chest, and the annoyed expression of someone who wasn't expecting anyone.

"Can I help you?" he asked.

Darn. Did she have the wrong day? No. She had checked her calendar and this appointment had definitely been scheduled for Wednesday. And it was Wednesday, wasn't it?

The man at the door gave her a wary look and held up his hands, both clad in dirt-caked gardening gloves. "If you're selling something, I'm not interested."

"No." She shook her head emphatically, trying to ignore his mucky gloves and struggling not to be distracted by the intensity of his eyes. Cool blue eyes that a girl could practically swim in. "I'm not selling anything."

"Who's she, Daddy?" the girl with the crooked pigtails asked before Kristi could continue.

"My name's Kristi." She smiled down at the adorable little girls, then extended her hand to their father. "Kristi Callahan. I have a two o'clock appointment to meet with the owners. The McTavishes?" Maybe she had the wrong address. "I'm the interior decorator with Ready Set Sold. You hired my company to stage your home and set up the real estate listing."

His expression went from accusatory to apologetic and he slapped a hand to his forehead—apparently forgetting about the gloves as he remembered the appointment—and applied a grimy streak to his brow.

She stared at it, contemplated the protocol with strangers who had spinach in their teeth, toilet paper stuck to a shoe, dirt on their faces, and decided there wasn't one.

He must have realized what she was looking at because he gave his forehead a hasty swipe with his forearm. The streak blurred to a smudge.

Kristi fought off a smile and lowered her gaze to the two little girls, who now flanked the man, each with an arm wound around a kneecap. The one was still sucking her thumb.

"Right. I'm Nate McTavish." He held out his hand, jerked it back and pulled off the glove. His handshake was confident, firm but not too firm. His skin was warm and, given the state of his gardening gloves, surprisingly dirt-free. "Your company was recommended by a colleague of mine. I plan to sell but the house needs some work and I wouldn't know where to start."

"I see." She noted that he said "I" rather than "we," and the little girls had already indicated their mother wasn't here. The hand that might give a clue to his marital status was still inside a gardening glove. *Not that it's any of your business,* she reminded herself, and tried to ease her hand out of his.

He quickly let go.

She dug a business card out of her bag and handed it to him, wishing her partner Claire had come instead. She always knew how to handle awkward situations.

"If this is a bad time—"

"No, not at all. I've been working in my greenhouse this afternoon and I lost track of the time."

In a way it was good that he hadn't been expecting her. She didn't have to apologize for being late.

"As I said, I'm the company's interior decorator. I help our clients get organized prior to listing their homes, assist with any decluttering or downsizing that might be needed. We'll work together to create a design plan to suit your home and your budget. Samantha Elliott, one of my partners, is a carpenter and she'll take care of any repairs or remodeling that has to be done. My other partner, Claire DeAngelo, is a real estate agent," she added, striving to sound polished and professional. "She handles the appraisal, the listing, arranges the open house, that sort of thing."

"This sounds like exactly what I need. I don't have much time for these kinds of things."

Kristi's initial uncertainty faded, but she forced herself to take a breath and slow the flow of information. "We take care of everything. I'm here today to take a look around and get an idea of what needs to be done and we'll take it from there. Um…will your wife be joining us?"

His earlier wariness was back, and if anything it was intensified. "No. She's…" He glanced down at his children and gently eased the thumb out of his daughter's mouth. "My wife passed away two years ago."

"Oh, I'm sorry. If there's anything I can—" *Stop. You don't offer to help a complete stranger.* "I'm so sorry."

"Thank you." Except he didn't sound grateful. He sounded as though he wished people would stop asking where his wife was, and stop offering clichéd condolences when they found out.

The little girl with the crooked pigtails tugged on his hand. "What's she doing here, Daddy?"

The other child had already recaptured her thumb.

"She's going to help us sell the house."

"Why?"

"Because we're going to move into a new one."

"Why?"

Kristi was reminded of her own daughter at this age, when the answer to every question generated another, especially when the answer was *because.* Creating a distraction had been the only way to make the questions stop.

"What are your names?" she asked.

"I'm Molly. She's Martha. We're sisters."

"Nice to meet you, Molly and Martha. How old are you?"

"Four." Molly appeared to be the pair's designated spokesperson.

Martha held up the four fingers of her free hand, apparently happy to let her sister do the talking.

They were adorable. They were also a poignant reminder of how much she loved children, how she'd never really got past the disappointment of not having more of her own. The panting dog nudged her elbow with its moist nose, making her laugh. She rubbed the top of its head in response.

"You should come in." Nate reached for the dog's collar and backed away from the door, taking the girls and the dog with him. "Sorry, I shouldn't have kept you standing out there."

"Thank you." She'd begun to wonder when that would occur to him. She stepped into the foyer and tripped over the fourth yellow rubber boot.

Stupid high-heeled shoes. She'd put them on, thinking they made her look more professional, and instead they turned her into a klutz.

Nate grabbed her elbow and held on till she'd regained her footing. She looked up and connected with his intense blue-eyed gaze, and for a second or two, or ten, she couldn't draw a breath. He was gorgeous.

When the clock started ticking again, he abruptly let her go, as though he'd read her thoughts, maybe even had similar ones of his own, and then with one foot he slid the boot out of her path. The dog snapped it up by the heel and gave it a shake, sending a spatter of drool across the floor.

Kristi shuddered.

"Girls, remember what we talked about? You need to put your things in the closet."

"That's Martha's," Molly said. "Mine are outside."

Martha tugged the boot out of the dog's mouth, tossed it onto the pile of things in the bottom of the closet and tried unsuccessfully to close the bifold door. She was remarkably adept at doing things with one hand.

"Sorry about the mess," Nate said. "If I had remembered you were coming, I would have tidied up."

Kristi couldn't tell if the closet door wouldn't close because the pile of clothing and footwear was in the way or if a hinge was broken, or both. She made a mental note to have Sam take a look at it, and added storage baskets to the list already forming in her head. She lived with a teenage girl and a dog so she knew a thing or two about clutter. At least the slate tile floor was clean, which, given the amount of traffic generated by two small children and one large dog, was a good sign. This man must be a decent housekeeper, or maybe he had a cleaning service. Either option scored him some points. The children looked well cared for, too, and in the grand scheme of things they were most important.

All this made Nate McTavish pretty much the opposite of the deadbeat dads in her life. That, along with his offhand charm and those heart-stopping eyes, should elevate her opinion of him. Instead the combination set off a loud clamor of mental alarm bells.

Get over yourself. Quiver-inducing blue eyes aside, she was here to do a job, not strike up an unwelcome relationship with a client.

"Not a problem. That's why I'm here." And if the rest of the house was anything like the foyer, she had her work cut out for her.

"Where would you like to start?" he asked.

"Is this the living room?" she asked, pointing to a pair of mullioned glass doors. With the frosted glass, they looked more like Japanese rice paper than traditional French doors.

He hesitated, then reluctantly pushed them open. "It is. We almost never use it so I keep the doors closed."

Kristi surveyed the interior. The curtains were closed and the room was dark and cool. The vaulted cedar-plank ceiling was draped with yellow-and-mauve crepe paper and clusters of matching balloons. Several balloons appeared to have come loose and were now on the floor, looking a little deflated.

"We had the girls' birthday party here last week and I didn't get around to taking down the decorations. I'll be sure to do that tonight."

Martha clung to her father's hand but Molly scampered into the room and attempted a balloon toss. The massive dog lumbered in behind her. The yellow blob of a balloon slithered to the floor so the child stomped on it instead. When it didn't pop, she lost interest and rejoined her father and sister. The dog nudged it with its nose, picked it up and gave it a chomp. Still no pop, so the Saint dropped the slobbery mass in the middle of the sisal area rug.

The room was furnished with comfortable-looking furniture and there was an abundance of books and newspapers, a few kids' toys and dog toys, and sofa cushions that needed straightening.

Kristi took her camera out of her bag and looped the strap around her neck. "If it's okay with you, I'd like to photograph each room. When I get back to my place… my office—" He didn't need to know she did most of her work out of the back of her minivan and at one end of her kitchen table. "The photographs help me create a design plan and draw up a budget."

"Fine with me. Are you okay to look around on your own? I still have some work to do outside." He pulled his gardening gloves back on.

"You go ahead," she said. "I'll look through the house and we can talk when I'm done."

"And I will tidy up in here tonight," he assured her again.

The week-old remnants of the party seemed to embarrass him. Kristi didn't see them as a problem, quite the opposite. At least there had been a party, and that was definitely to his credit. She couldn't remember the last time Jenna's dad had even called to wish their daughter a happy birthday. Gifts? Not even a consideration.

"Molly. Martha. Let's go. You can play outside while I work."

"Daddy, why is she taking pictures?"

"She needs to know what the house looks like."

He took Molly's hand and coaxed her out of the room along with her sister, who needed no urging at all. The dog seemed content to amble along after them.

"Why?"

"Because."

"Because why?"

"Because she just does."

To say Nate McTavish was overwhelmed by single-parenthood would be the understatement of the century, but what he lacked in technique, he made up for with patience. In spades.

As he walked away, she smiled at the green lettering on the back of his T-shirt. Go Green With Photosynthesis. At least now the equation on the front made sense, and confirmed her guess that he probably was a gardener. Her gaze dropped a little lower. There was a lot to be said for a flattering pair of jeans, but these particular jeans were simply magic. She quickly looked away. *You have a job to do, and* that *is not it.*

Since her ex, Derek the Deadbeat, had left twelve years

ago, she had been on a number of casual dates, mostly with men her family and friends had set her up with, but she had guarded against anything that would distract her from becoming a self-sufficient single mom and career woman.

Everything about this man was distracting. The hair that could use a trim but suited him anyway, his being oblivious to the streak of dirt on his forehead, and oh… those eyes. She never felt awkward with new clients, but if she'd had to go through every room in the house with him, knowing those eyes watched every move she made, she would not have been able to focus. Especially after the moment they'd had when she tripped over the little yellow boot. And it hadn't just been *her* moment. He'd felt it, too. She was sure of it.

With him out of the room if not entirely out of her mind, she pulled open the heavy drapes and imagined the clutter away. The rich wood of the floors and beamed ceiling created a warm contrast to the polished river rock of the open-hearth fireplace. She would start staging in this room, she decided. The fireplace was the focal point of the room, and it would create the perfect jumping-off point for the casual West Coast decor she would carry throughout the house. She didn't even need to see the other rooms to know she could make it work.

She raised her camera, snapped a photo of the fireplace and then systematically documented the rest of the room.

Her BlackBerry buzzed before she had a chance to move on. It was her mother. She could either take the call now or wade through a half dozen messages later on. Kristi adored her mom, but in the history of motherhood, Gwen Callahan's persistence in checking up on her daughter was unmatched.

"Hi, Mom. What's up?"

"Hello, dear. I hope I'm not interrupting anything."

"Actually, I'm in the middle of a job."

"Oh. Well then, this'll just take a minute."

I suppose there's a first time for everything. "What would you like?"

"I was just talking to my old friend, Cathie Halverson. You remember her, don't you? They lived across the street when you were in high school, then they moved to Spokane."

"Ye-e-e-e-s." Kristi already knew where this was going.

"Her son Bernard has just moved back to Seattle. I'm sure you remember him."

All too well. Bernie Halverson had asked her to a school dance when she was fifteen. She went because it was the first time anyone had ever asked her out and she hadn't had the sense to say no. The date had been a disaster. They'd had nothing to talk about, and his idea of slow-dancing was synonymous with groping. He had reeked of cheap cologne, and the next day she'd had to wash her favorite sweater three times to get the smell out of it. But the worst part had definitely been the kiss.

"Sure," she said. "I sort of remember him."

"He doesn't know that many people in Seattle," Gwen said. "So I was thinking we could invite him to Aunt Wanda and Uncle Ted's Fourth of July barbecue. Doesn't that sound like a good idea?"

To Bernie Halverson, it might. For a split second she considered telling her mother he'd been the first boy to stick his tongue in her mouth, she hadn't liked it one bit and if he was still single after all these years it's because he was still a letch.

She couldn't tell her mother that. Gwen Callahan did not like to discuss "intimacies," as she so delicately referred to them. But then straight out of the blue, Kristi had a better idea.

"I don't think so, Mom. I've actually just met some-one." It wasn't a lie, really. She had just met *someone*. Nate McTavish. So it was only the teeniest of lies. Just a fib, really. "It's nothing serious or anything but I don't think we should give Bernie...Bernard...the wrong idea."

It took her mother five full seconds to respond. "You're seeing someone? When did this happen? Why haven't you said anything? Has Jenna met him? Are the two of you—"

"Mom, stop. It's recent, very recent, and like I said, it hasn't turned into anything serious. And no, Jenna hasn't met him so I'd appreciate it if you didn't say anything to her."

"What's his name? What does he do?"

"Oh. Nate. His name's Nate and he's a... He works in landscaping." And in a blink the fib turned into a terrible lie that she would, without question, live to regret.

"Well, this is certainly a surprise. Where did you meet him?"

"Through work." That part was true. "And I'm at work right now, Mom, so I really can't talk."

"I'll call you tonight so we can make plans. You'll have to invite him to Wanda's barbecue so we can all meet him. So Jenna can meet him. Or you can give me his number and I'll invite him."

And there came the part where she would live to regret this...right on schedule. "No! No. Thanks, Mom. I'll talk to him about it. I'm not sure if he's free, though. I think maybe he mentioned something about having plans with his family." *Stop. Talking.* The hole she was digging would soon be so deep, she'd never climb out of it. "I have to go, Mom. I'm working with a new client this afternoon. I'll talk to you later."

"I'll call you tonight," Gwen said again.

Kristi couldn't tell if there was a subtle threat in her

mother's parting words, or if the guilt she was feeling had
skewed her perception. Most likely a little of both.

Over the years her mother and Aunt Wanda had tried
to set her up with more eligible men than she could count.
She'd managed to avoid going out with most of them, but
occasionally they'd caught her off guard, like the times
they had invited someone like Bernie Halverson to a family event. Not one of those men had come close to looking
like Nate McTavish. Not that looks were everything, but
there hadn't been any chemistry with any of them, either.
Shaking hands with Nate had left her insides bubbling like
a beaker over a Bunsen burner.

Even his T-shirt has chemistry written all over it.

She rolled her eyes at that thought. She had no business getting all dreamy-eyed schoolgirl over her new client. She had a job to do.

From somewhere in the house, a phone rang. She
counted six rings before it stopped, unanswered.

She quickly scrolled through her photographs of the living room. Satisfied she had everything she needed for now,
she crossed the room, opened a second set of frosted glass
doors and walked into the dining room. Another unused
space, judging by the cool temperature and drifts of gift
wrap and empty toy packaging littering the floor. There
were more yellow-and-mauve streamers and dejected-
looking balloons, but everything else about the dining
room was neat as a pin. It was spacious, with plenty of
room to maneuver around a table that would comfortably
seat ten. The furniture was a little too flea-market-finds-
meet-grandma's-attic to really suit the house, but some of it
was solid and in good condition. She always liked to keep
her budget as low as possible, so she would make it work.

From the moment she'd driven up, she'd loved this
house, but now she felt a little sad for it, having its beau-

tiful rooms closed up and uninhabited. This house deserved to be lived in by someone who would love it at least as much as she did.

At the back of the dining room was a third pair of opaque glass doors, closed like the others. She pulled them open, stepped into a spacious and *very* messy kitchen, tripped over the dog's water bowl and sent a small tidal wave gushing across the tile floor.

"Oh, for heaven's sake. Who puts a bowl of water in front of a closed door?" Apparently a frazzled single dad did. She had no idea where to look for a mop and she couldn't leave this huge puddle on the kitchen floor. So much for working through the house on her own. Now she had to find that distractingly sexy and very single dad and ask him for help.

Chapter Two

Nate herded the girls and the dog through the family room.

"Why can't we stay with the lady?" Molly asked.

"Because I have work to do."

"We can stay with her."

"She has work to do, too," he said, sliding the patio door open.

"Taking pictures?"

"Yes." And he was happy to leave her on her own. It was one thing to stand with her in the living room, or almost any other room, while she made notes and took photographs. But eventually they would get to his bedroom, and the idea of going in there with her had brought on a mild state of panic.

"She has a pretty purse," Molly said.

"Does she?" He shut the patio door behind them. He had only noticed her bag was huge. And stuffed full.

"It has cupcakes on it."

"Does it?"

Martha pulled her thumb out of her mouth. "I yike cupcakes."

"I know you *like* cupcakes. Why don't you two go in the playhouse and have a look at the new dress-up clothes Aunt Britt dropped off this morning." He'd asked Britt to bring them out here because the girls' bedroom already looked like Toys "R" Us had tangled with a tornado. "Maybe she brought you some purses."

His sister, a self-proclaimed clotheshorse, frequently cleared out her closet to make room for new things and bestowed the items she no longer wanted on her nieces. The girls loved it, but their bedroom, the family room and now the playhouse overflowed with toys and Britt's cast-offs.

"Come on, Martha. Let's see what she brung us." Molly snagged the dog by the collar and tugged. "You, too, Gemmy."

At the entrance to the playhouse, she let go of the Saint's collar and skipped inside. Martha straggled in behind her, and Gemmy sprawled across the doorway, head resting on her paws.

After they were settled, Nate turned his attention to the rows of potted asters in his makeshift greenhouse and tried not to think about the beautiful woman with the ginormous cupcake purse who was discovering that he was not the world's greatest housekeeper. How had he not remembered to put a reminder about this meeting in his calendar? If he had, he would have spent last evening tidying up instead of going over the final draft of his current research paper.

He measured the height of a plant and recorded the data in the spreadsheet on his laptop.

Kristi Callahan was stunning in a wholesome girl-next-door sort of way, with a lively swing to her blond ponytail and an engaging flash in her gray-green eyes. More green than gray. She smelled good, too.

His cell phone rang. After three rings, he tracked it to the end of the workbench, where it was hiding beneath a spare pair of gloves. His in-laws' phone number was displayed on the screen. What now?

"Hello, Alice. How are you?"

"Nate, I was getting worried. I called the house but no one answered."

Nate sighed. He and the kids could have been out for the afternoon or even just at the supermarket, and he refused to check in with her every time they left the house.

"Sorry, Alice. I didn't hear it ringing. I'm out in the greenhouse."

"Where are the girls?"

He resented the accusatory tone. Where did she think they were? "They're in the playhouse. Gemmy and I are keeping an eye on them."

"That's good. You know if you're busy, you can drop them off here anytime. Fred and I are always happy to see them."

There were lots of things he'd like to say, but only one of them was polite. "Thank you. I appreciate that."

"Did that person from the real estate company show up?"

Now they were getting to the real reason for her call. At least she'd called and not shown up unannounced as she often did. He never should have told her he was going to sell the house, especially since her constant interference was one of his reasons for wanting to move. He didn't like the idea of being too far from the university, but his next house would be a lot farther than fourteen blocks from Alice and Fred's.

"She's taking a look at the house right now."

"And you're out in the greenhouse?"

"I wanted to keep Gemmy and the girls out of her way, so I brought them outside. Besides, she's just deciding what needs to be done." He didn't have to be around for that.

"You should have asked us to help instead of spending good money to have someone else do this."

Nate closed his eyes and, for several seconds, indulged

in the idea of applying for a faculty position at another university. One on the other side of the country. Or maybe in a different country.

"There's a house for sale down the street from us," Alice said. "It would be perfect for you and the girls, and they're having an open house on the weekend. You should come by and have a look."

"That sounds…interesting." Nate picked up a garden trowel and imagined stabbing himself in the head with it. Alice had lost her only child, he reminded himself, but that didn't make it easy for him to rationalize her interference. After Heather died, Alice had transferred all of her attention to her granddaughters. Understandable, and he appreciated everything she did for them. Mostly. But she had always made it clear that she considered him to be partly responsible for Heather's death. He'd managed to heap a fair amount of blame on himself and he didn't need her adding to it. She was Molly and Martha's grandmother and he had to be civil, but no way was he buying a house within walking distance of the world's most meddlesome mother-in-law. He set the trowel on his workbench.

"While I have you on the phone," Alice continued. "Remember that children's beauty pageant we discussed?"

His insides coiled into a knot. There had been no discussion. Only her saying he should enter the girls, and him saying no. "Yes, I remember."

"You might not like the idea, but you should look at their website before you make up your mind. It will be so good for them."

Good for them? They were four years old.

"Especially Martha," she said. "These sorts of things build confidence and that will help her to stop sucking her thumb."

"I've been busy, Alice."

"The application deadline is only a couple of weeks away."

He contemplated the trowel again. "Right. I'll take a look." Or not. There was no way *his* daughters would be paraded around like a pair of miniature beauty queens, not to mention having to compete with one another. No way in hell.

"Speaking of the girls," he said, not wanting to leave her with another opening. "I need to check on them. Thanks for calling, Alice. I'll talk to you later."

He set his phone on the table and stared at it, picturing it impaled by the garden trowel. Instead he measured the next plant and updated the spreadsheet while he shoved the conversation with Alice to the back of his mind. He had more important, and appealing, things to think about. Like the woman currently inside his home.

He could kick himself for forgetting she was coming here this afternoon. A colleague at the university had recommended Ready Set Sold, so he had called them from his office and scrawled the appointment on a notepad, which by now was buried on his desk beneath everything else he'd been working on—the syllabus for the summer school course he was teaching next month, a draft of a research paper he was coauthoring with a colleague and the latest edition of the *American Journal of Botany*. He really needed to be better organized, but he could scarcely remember a time when his life wasn't out of control.

In the months after his wife died, he had welcomed the help and support he'd received. Even relied on it. Over time, his family had backed off, but not Heather's. They meant well, at least that's what he wanted to believe, but their good intentions frequently overstepped the boundaries. Without coming right out and saying it, Alice often implied that he should be doing a better job of raising her granddaughters, of keeping the house tidier, of being two parents instead of just one.

She insisted Molly and Martha were old enough to look after their own things, and part of him acknowledged that might be true, but he couldn't bring himself to make them do it. They had already lost their mother, so it didn't seem right that they be stuck with an overbearing father who made them earn their keep. Alice was also of the opinion that Martha was too old to be sucking her thumb, and she was now pressuring him to put an end to that by entering her in a beauty pageant of all things.

Heather would have known exactly how to handle her mother and their daughters. Why didn't he? He was a bright guy with a PhD and a career as a scientist. When it came to family, he felt hopelessly in over his head, and he was also smart enough to know that reflected his own upbringing. His mother had kept house and raised him and his sister. His father had been the family's sole bread-winner and his fallback approach to child rearing had always been "go ask your mother." Over the years Nate had learned a lot of things from his dad, but parenting skills weren't among them.

These days Nate rarely thought about the weeks and months after Heather died, leaving him with a pair of toddlers and a fledgling career as a professor of botany at the University of Washington. When he did reflect on those dark days, they were blurred by grief, and even a little guilt. His two-year-old daughters had needed his undivided attention, 24/7, and that had kept him going. The university had even granted him a semester's leave. Many people, including his family and Heather's, thought he should have taken more time off but he had wanted to get his life back to normal.

Now, two years later, he was probably as adept at juggling his family and his professional life as he would ever be, and it felt as though the ship had sailed on establishing boundaries for his in-laws. Selling the house and moving to another neighborhood might not be the best solution, but right now it felt like his only one. And it was better to do it now. The girls wouldn't stay little forever. They'd be starting school next year, and this would get easier. It had to.

He knew the future would bring different demands, not fewer, but a smaller house would be more manageable, and a fresh start might make it easier to lay down some new ground rules. But first he had to sell this house, and he was definitely smart enough to know he needed professional help with that. Heather had planned to decorate right after they bought the place, but she was already pregnant, and then she got sick. The girls were born six weeks early, and then she got even sicker. Curtains and cushions had never been on his list of priorities, and they had dropped off Heather's. Once he'd made the decision to sell the house, Ready Set Sold seemed like the perfect solution. Alice might think "home staging" was a waste of money and phony as hell, but Kristi Callahan seemed like the real deal. Even her blond hair looked natural. Nice curves, great legs—

"Nate?"

He dropped his calipers.

"I'm sorry," Kristi said. "I didn't mean to startle you."

"Oh. No, you didn't." Like hell she didn't. His imagination had been on the verge of conducting a closer examination of those legs. He hoped his red face didn't give that away. "I'm just clumsy," he lied.

Her laugh sounded completely genuine. "Clumsy is my middle name. I'm afraid I spilled your dog's water bowl. It was in front of the door between the dining room and the kitchen, and I can't find anything to clean it up."

He bent down to pick up the calipers, came face-to-knee with the hem of her skirt and jolted himself back to the upright position. "Don't worry about it. I'll come in and mop it up."

"So, this is your greenhouse," she said, looking around. "It's not what I expected."

"It's technically not a greenhouse. It was built as a pergola and the previous owners converted it into a pool house by adding the change room at the back. We don't use the swimming pool." He gestured at the bright blue cover. "So I closed this in with heavy-gauge plastic and use it as a greenhouse instead."

"I see."

He could tell she didn't, but at least she hadn't called it an eyesore like his mother-in-law had.

"You have a lot of plants," she said. "Is this what you do for a living?"

He surveyed the rows of asters. "I teach botany at Washington U. I'm collecting data for a senior undergraduate course I'll be teaching this fall."

"So, you're a university professor." She was still looking at the plants as though she wasn't quite sure what to make of them.

"Yes, and I also do research." Oh, geez. As if she would care.

"What are you researching?" she asked, probably because she felt she had to say something.

"The poor reproductive barriers in species of angiosperms."

"Really?" She looked puzzled. "I didn't think plants had sperm."

Nate laughed. "I said *angio*sperms. That's the botanical term for flowering plants. You're right that plants don't have sperm. At least not in the strictest sense of the word."

Her cheeks flared pink. Her comment had been inno-cent enough and he wished he had let it go.

"I thought you might be a gardener," she said.

Now it was his turn to be puzzled.

"You were wearing garden gloves when you answered the door and your T-shirt—" She glanced at his chest and away again. "So…"

He liked that she was still blushing.

"It's the equation for photosynthesis," he said. "I got this at a conference I attended last year."

"I thought so. I mean, that's what it says on the back. So, about the mop…" She hiked her thumb toward the house. "I need to clean up the water I spilled and finish looking through the other rooms."

He also liked that she was outwardly more flustered than he felt on the inside. "I'll clean it up. It's my fault for leaving Gemmy's bowl in front of the door."

He set the calipers beside the next plant he needed to measure, saved the spreadsheet and closed his laptop. "Molly? Martha? I'm going inside for a couple of minutes."

"We're playing school," Molly yelled back. "An' I'm the teacher."

"Good for you. I'll be right back. Gemmy, stay," he said, giving the dog the palm-out signal for "stay." She rolled onto her side with her back firmly pressed against the playhouse door and her eyelids slowly slid shut. She wasn't going anywhere and neither were the girls.

"I take it Gemmy is a girl," Kristi said as they circled the pool together and walked toward the house.

"She is. It's short for Hegemone."

"That's an unusual name. I've never heard it before."

"Hegemone is the Greek goddess of plants. The botany connection seemed like a good idea when I got her. Then the girls came along and they couldn't pronounce it so they shortened it to Gemmy. She also responds to Gem. And Milk-Bone treats."

"My dog's name is Hercules. That's a Greek god, too. I think."

"Roman, actually. Borrowed from the Greek Heracles, son of Zeus. He was half mortal and half god."

"Oh. We thought he was the god of strength or something."

She wasn't wearing a wedding ring so he'd assumed she was single. The "we" implied otherwise.

"He was, among other things," Nate said. He resisted the urge to elaborate. She probably already thought he was a complete nerd. No point sounding like a walking encyclopedia and removing any doubt. "What kind of dog is Hercules?"

"A Yorkshire terrier."

He laughed. "Good name. Does he live up to it?"

He slid the patio door open for her and waited for her to go inside.

"Only in that he has me and my daughter completely wrapped around one of his tiny little paws."

"But not your husband?"

She met his gaze head-on. "I don't have a husband."

"I see." He had wanted it to sound like an innocent question. It was anything but, and they both knew it. For a few seconds they stared awkwardly at one another, then she looked away.

"So…I'll just grab the mop."

He left her waiting in the family room and sidestepped the massive puddle on the kitchen floor. He looked in several places before he located the mop in the mudroom and the bucket in the garage.

In the kitchen, Kristi stood at the end of the penin-sula that separated the kitchen from the eating area. She had set her enormous cupcake bag on the counter next to her and was looking at the monitor of the camera in her hands. The bag was a light purple color and printed with wildly colorful cupcakes, which the girls had gushed over. It was also large and completely stuffed. He'd heard all the jokes about the contents of a woman's handbag, but this was over-the-top. How much stuff did one woman need to carry around with her?

"You have a great house," she said, without looking up from the camera.

"Thanks." *You have great legs,* he thought as he quickly looked down and up again, past the purple skirt and short, matching jacket with the big black buttons, relieved she wasn't watching him.

He set the bucket on the floor, and Kristi reached for the mop.

He shook his head. "I'll look after it. It was my fault anyway. I keep the door closed, so I put the water there because it was out of the way."

As he ran the mop over the floor, he kept a surreptitious eye on Kristi. She wasn't paying any attention to him. Instead something on the fridge door had caught her attention. The latest strip of pictures of him and the girls from the photo booth at the mall.

"Cute photographs," she said.

"Thanks. We started taking them when their—" *When their mother was dying.* Daily visits to the hospital had become too much of a strain for her and too stressful for the girls, so he'd started taking the photographs to her instead. He couldn't tell that to a stranger. "We started taking them a couple of years ago. It's sort of become a tradition."

"I think it's lovely," she said.

He worked the mop across the floor, keeping what seemed like a safe distance from her. Safe, that is, until his gaze sought out the shapely curve of her calves, the slender ankles....

The mop handle connected with something.

He whipped around in time to see her enormous cupcake bag slide off the counter, but he was too slow to catch it. Like a slice of buttered toast, it flipped and hit the floor upside down, and then there was no need to wonder what was in the bag because its contents were strewn across the damp kitchen floor. "Dammit."

Kristi set her camera on the counter, laughed and knelt at the same time he did, the tip of her blond ponytail brushing the side of his face as she tossed it over her shoulder. She smelled like springtime and lilacs.

She started cramming her possessions back into the bag.

He gathered as many things as he could and handed them to her. A notebook, several pens, an empty Tic Tac box, a hairbrush, two tampons and...oh, geez...a condom? The warmth of a flush crept up his neck, but he was sure his red face was no match for hers. She held the bag open and he dropped everything inside, avoiding eye contact.

"Thanks." She stuffed a bunch of receipts and a wallet into the bag. "I think we got everything."

He stood up, and she stood up, wobbling a little on account of her heels. He grasped her arm to steady her, reminded of how she'd nearly tripped on Martha's boot. She smiled up at him, and when he looked into the depths of her green eyes he felt like a cliff diver plunging headfirst into an unfamiliar sea.

"So..." she said, then stopped as though she wasn't sure what else to say. A lot of her sentences started that way.

"I should get back outside. The girls are out there, and I still have work to do."

"Me, too." She flung the overstuffed bag over her shoulder. "Inside, not outside. It won't take me long to finish up, then I was thinking I could just let myself out. Would it be okay if I come back tomorrow? In the morning, maybe, say around nine, if you're not too busy. That'll give me a chance to look through the photos I've taken, talk to my partners." She stopped, drew a long breath.

She was embarrassed, probably in a hurry to get out of here, and it was his fault. If he'd been paying attention to what he was doing instead of admiring her legs, he wouldn't have knocked her bag off the counter. And then, if he'd been paying attention, he would have left the little plastic packet for her to pick up and pretended not to see it.

Now the stupid condom had become the elephant in the room—

The bad analogy practically had him groaning out loud.

"Tomorrow morning's good," he said. "Nine o'clock. I was planning to work at home anyway."

"Great. I'll put together a proposal tonight and we can discuss it then."

She reached for her camera, and as she got close he backed away, sensing it was a bad idea to get *too* close to a woman who smelled like a cross between an English country garden and a Hollywood starlet's boudoir. Not that he knew anything about the latter, but he was a man after all, and he did have an imagination. She must have been thinking the same thing…about getting too close… because she hastily backed away, too.

"Thanks. And, um, I'm sorry about the water, and for taking you away from your work. I'm usually not *this* clumsy."

He didn't believe her. In spite of her polished appearance she seemed to have a knack for running into things, tripping over them. Oddly, it made her even more captivating. He had no business being captivated, though.

She might not have a husband, but the condom in her bag meant she was involved with someone. And if she wasn't… well, he didn't want to know what it meant.

"Is there anything else I can tell you about the house?" he asked, not knowing what else to say.

"I don't think so. I'll just take a quick look at the bedrooms and let myself out. I assume they're down the hallway off the foyer."

He nodded.

She whirled around and once again his nose filled with her heavenly scent.

She crossed the family room like it was a runway, the flippy hem of her skirt flirting with her knees and the heels of her shoes making a crisp, sharp sound against the hardwood. Just before she left the room, she smiled at him over her shoulder, as if to say she knew perfectly well why he was still standing there.

"See you in the morning." And then she was gone.

You're wasting your time, he told himself. *She's not your type.*

Did he even have a type? He'd thought it was Heather. She had been every bit as attractive as this woman was, just in a more down-to-earth, practical way. No swirly skirts and purple cupcake bags for her. Heather had been studiously working toward a doctorate in psychology when they'd started dating. They hadn't talked about marriage, but it was the obvious thing to do after they'd found out they were expecting.

The pregnancy had taken a heavy toll on Heather's health, but then the girls arrived and they seemed like such a gift, such a natural extension of their lives that neither of them had given much thought to any scenario other than Heather getting better. She hadn't.

He'd been left with a lot of questions. Would she have

married him under any other circumstances? Would he have married her? Those were questions with no answers, only regrets. Would she still be alive if not for the pregnancy? Of course she would. It took two people to make a baby and the rational scientific part of his brain knew that. The part that housed his conscience was another matter. It ate at him with a relentless appetite.

As for the beautiful woman who had just disappeared down the hallway, the one who might be walking into his bedroom at that precise moment, he had questions. Truth was he shouldn't have any, but that wouldn't prevent him from looking forward to seeing her tomorrow morning and maybe getting the answers to some of them.

Chapter Three

The next morning Kristi yawned and poured herself a cup of tea, then settled in at the kitchen table with her laptop. She had stayed up far too late last night, going over the photographs of Nate McTavish's house and drafting a design plan. She was not a morning person at the best of times, and agreeing to meet him at nine o'clock had been a bad idea. Now she had just over an hour to review her proposal, check her email and make the twenty-minute drive to the university district.

Hercules nosed her ankle. He sat on his haunches and cocked his head when she smiled down at him.

"Hey, Herc. Do you want to sit with me?"

He danced on his hind legs, tail wagging, and she swept him onto her lap. From beneath shaggy brows, his black-button eyes sparkled up at her.

"Sit and be good or I'll put you down."

He settled in, and Kristi opened her email.

She wrapped one hand around her teacup and breathed in the heady jasmine-scented steam rising from it. After a quick scan of her in-box, she clicked on a message from her business partner Claire DeAngelo.

Thanks for sharing your photographs and design plan for the McTavish house. Love your ideas! Knowing

you, the place will be organized in no time. Let's see what Sam says about the renos you've suggested. The "greenhouse" definitely has to go, but the professor looks like a keeper. C.
PS: remember our 10:30 conference call.

The message ended with the emoticon for a wink.

Very funny, Kristi thought. She had wanted Sam to see the pergola–pool house structure that Nate had converted into a greenhouse, but she shouldn't have sent a picture with him in it.

She opened a folder on her desktop and clicked to open the photograph.

Turning the structure back into a pool house wouldn't take much work, so there was really no justifying the amount of time she'd spent studying the photo last night. Claire was right. He looked ridiculously good. If anyone had asked her to imagine what a botany professor looked like, her imagination would have conjured up the exact opposite of this tall, fit-without-being-totally-ripped man with gorgeous eyes and a killer smile.

She quickly clicked to close the image and opened Sam's email next.

I agree with Claire. Great house. Great ideas. Definitely looking forward to meeting your Professor Hottie. S.

Sam's email ended with two winks.

Oh, for heaven's sake. Their comments were all in good fun, but Kristi rolled her eyes as she read them. She had given some sketchy background information on their new client when she'd sent the photographs and the proposal to her partners late last night. Sketchy details were all she knew. He was a single dad and a widower who found that one big house and two small girls were more than he could juggle with his demanding career.

Claire, recently separated and almost certainly headed for divorce court, had declared she was off the market. Besides, Nate wasn't her type. Her ex was an investment broker with a taste for money and a penchant for keeping up appearances. Kristi had never liked him, had always thought Claire could do better, but her friend was totally type A when it came to organizing her life. Nate's disorganization would drive her crazy.

Sam and the love of her life, recently married at a quiet ceremony with a small gathering of family and close friends, wouldn't give another man a second glance, no matter how hot he happened to be. Kristi had been thrilled to share maid of honor duties with Claire, and they couldn't be happier that their business partner was happily settled with her husband AJ and their young son, Will.

Claire's and Sam's teasing was strictly for Kristi's benefit. That they had picked up on her immediate attraction to this man was a testament to how well they knew one another. They also knew she was determined to maintain control of her life, at least until her daughter was grown-up and off to college, and that meant not having a man in it.

Her deadbeat dad had abandoned her and her mother after he'd lost his job, remortgaged their home and gambled everything away. And then she'd made the same mistake her mother had. Let herself be swept off her feet by a guy who was all talk and no substance. Got pregnant right out of high school. Married the guy because of course that was the right thing to do, and learned too late that he couldn't hold down a job, didn't know how to be a husband much less a dad and had no interest in learning.

Now her mission in life was to set an example for her daughter and break the cycle so Jenna didn't make the same mistake. Setting a good example meant not getting involved with a man, any man, but especially not another deadbeat, until Jenna was past the age of being impressionable.

Anyone could see that Nate McTavish was smart, decent, easy on the eyes and about as far from deadbeat as any man could be, but he was still a man. He had a lot going on in his life, including grieving the loss of his wife. Kristi would be the first to admit she had enough baggage of her own. To heck with taking on anyone else's.

Once more she scrolled through all the photographs she'd taken, from the living room and dining room with their festive party streamers to the cluttered kitchen where a board game on the table was still surrounded by lunch dishes that hadn't been cleared away.

One photo captured the refrigerator and a cluttered counter. Like hundreds of other homes, the front of the fridge was plastered with notes, calendars, kids' artwork. It was the photo booth strip that leaped out at her, though. She enlarged the photograph and leaned closer to the screen for a better look. Four images of Nate and his girls, snapped in rapid succession, laughing and grinning and making silly faces at the camera. Her chest went tight, the way it had when she'd first seen the pictures yesterday. There had been more strips on a tackboard in the girls' bedroom, one on Nate's dresser in the master bedroom and several on the desk in his home office. None of them, at least none that she'd seen, had included the wife and mother this family had lost, but together they created a poignant record of Nate's daughters as they grew up. Altogether she'd noticed eight or ten of the strips scattered throughout the house, and she felt sure she would encounter more as she drilled down through the layers of clutter.

Organizing a client's personal mementos fell well outside the kind of work she usually did, but the mother in her wanted to do something special with those photographs. She wished she had started a tradition like that when Jenna was little. Suggesting it now would yield one of her daughter's signature eye rolls and a "Mo-om, that's so lame."

Speaking of Jenna...

Kristi glanced at the clock. Darn. In a futile attempt to keep herself on track, she kept it set five minutes fast. Even deducting those precious minutes, they were running late and it was almost time for her daughter to leave for school.

She scooted Hercules off her lap and drained her teacup as she shut down her laptop and stuffed it into her bag along with the rest of her things. On her way through the kitchen she deposited her cup in the sink and hauled her bag to the bench by the front door. Now to find her keys.

"Jenna?" she called up the stairs as she scanned the surface of the small console table inside the front door. "Are you ready?"

"Almost. Do you know where my iPod is?" Jenna shouted back.

Kristi put her search for her missing keys on pause. *Exactly where you left it,* she thought. *Ditto for my keys.*

"Haven't seen it, sweetie." And she didn't have time to look. Her daughter could survive for one day without Justin and Selena. She, on the other hand, couldn't get her day started until she found her keys.

She should have taken less time going through photos, less time checking email and a lot less time fussing with her hair and makeup. Then she had put on her blue sneakers, realized they were scuffed and grimy from clearing out a previous client's garage and changed to the pink ones. But her blue T-shirt didn't go, so she changed to a white one, decided against it and dashed downstairs to retrieve a pink shirt from the dryer. Then she'd let herself get distracted and had folded the rest of the laundry and put it away.

How she managed to stay on task in a client's home while being so disorganized in her own was a constant source of frustration for her…and an endless source of amusement for Sam and Claire. And now, because of it, she was going to be late.

Back in the kitchen she picked up a dish towel to see if her keys were hiding beneath it. They weren't. This was rapidly turning into one of those mornings when nothing went the way she wanted it to. She quickly folded the towel, hung it on the handle of the oven door, moved on to the dining room table. No keys on the half she used as her office. The other end was Jenna's homework space, and the two halves met in the middle in a muddle of personal items, assorted junk mail and a pair of hurricane candle lanterns, placed there to create a little ambience after their last cleaning session.

No sense looking there. Had she put the keys in her bag? Claire, the poster girl for organized efficiency, had suggested attaching a lanyard to the strap of her handbag and clipping her keys to that when she wasn't using them. An excellent suggestion and it had worked like a charm, until she'd switched purses and didn't transfer the orange lanyard because it didn't match the purple bag. *Note to self. Buy a lanyard to match every bag.*

She retrieved her bag from the front hall and set it on the kitchen counter. Wallet, makeup bag, lint roller, dog leash, but no keys. She shoved those items aside and dumped the rest onto the counter. The loose contents included a handful of spare change, two Milk-Bone treats, the tube of lipstick she'd hunted for earlier that morning… and one condom.

She picked it up and stared at it, recalling in excruciat-

ing detail Nate McTavish's embarrassment when he'd realized what he had in his hand. She had been every bit as
mortified. Did he think she was one of those women who
was always ready for a little action? Ugh. Nothing could
be further from the truth. She avoided as many blind dates
as possible, and the only action she saw when she did date
was never more than an awkward good-night kiss. No
condom needed.

Yesterday she had been even more embarrassed when
Nate told her about his research. Something about poor
reproductive barriers in flowering plants. She still didn't
completely understand what he'd been talking about, even
though she'd tried to look it up on the internet last night.
He might as well have been talking Greek.

"For sure he was talking geek," she said, smiling at her
own cleverness.

Fourteen years ago she had learned the hard way that
at least one brand of condom had provided a very poor
barrier to reproduction. Thank goodness she hadn't re-
vealed that yesterday. Bad enough she'd blurted out some
nonsense about sperm. What had she been thinking? His
laugh had been a few registers lower than his speaking
voice, deep and sexy with a flash of perfect white teeth.
He might be a geek, but he was a darned sexy one.

Jenna thundered down the stairs. "Mom? Are you *sure*
you haven't seen it?"

Kristi shoved the small plastic packet into her bag and
hastily put everything else back on top of it. "Have I seen
what?"

"My *iPod.*"

Right. "No, I haven't."

"Well, crap."

"Excuse me?"

"'Crap' isn't swearing, Mom." Jenna dropped her backpack by the front door and glanced around the living room.

Kristi didn't have time to argue. "Do you remember what you were doing the last time you used it?"

"No. If I did…" Jenna was halfway across the room when she stopped. "Sleeping! I fell asleep listening to Katy Perry." She whirled around and dashed for the stairs. "I'll bet it's still in my bed. Thanks, Mom!"

"You're welcome." Now if only the same strategy would work for her. She had come home from work yesterday afternoon, brought in a handful of mail, picked up the paper…aha, that was it. She must've left her keys on the coffee table where she'd deposited everything else.

Sure enough, there they were, under the newspaper. Jenna had flipped it open to check the movie listings, not wanting to wait until Kristi had finished uploading photographs to her laptop so she could check them online. Being a typical teenager, she had used the inconvenience as an opportunity to bemoan the fact that she was stuck with her mother's retired cell phone instead of the iPhone she so desperately needed.

A car horn sounded in front of the town house and Jenna raced back down the stairs. "That's my car pool. Gotta go."

"I'll be home early," Kristi said, as much a warning to her daughter that she shouldn't bring boys home after school. One boy in particular. That strategy would work until next week when school let out for the summer. Then she wasn't sure how she would do her job and chaperone a teenager who was too old for a babysitter but too young to be left on her own all day.

"See ya later, Mom!"

"We're having pasta for dinner. If you could make a—" Her request that Jenna make a salad to go with it was cut off by the slam of the front door. She could leave her a note, but Jenna would say she didn't see it. Better to send her a text message. Teenagers *never* let a text go unread, and her daughter was no exception.

Kristi opened the door to their backyard patio and shooed Hercules outside. "Go on. Do your business, then I have to get out of here."

While he was outside, she checked her bag to be sure she had everything she needed for the day, then glanced at her watch. She hadn't packed a lunch, but if she left now she would only be a few minutes late. Ten minutes, max. She'd have to take a break at lunchtime and run out to grab a bite to eat, and that would waste more time. She opened the fridge and scooped up a couple of bottles of water, an apple and the makings of a cheese sandwich. Now she could work through lunch to make up for not being on time. She took out a plastic container filled with the cupcakes she had baked on the weekend. She hated to see them go to waste, and Nate and his daughters might like them.

"Come on, Herc." She picked him up when he scampered inside, gave him a scratch behind the ears and set him in his bed. "Keep an eye on Jenna when she gets home. I have to dash."

Worrying about being late was likely a waste of time, though. Nate McTavish didn't seem like the kind of guy who paid any attention to the clock. He probably wouldn't even notice that she was running a little behind.

NATE POURED HIMSELF a second cup of coffee and settled at the breakfast bar with his laptop. Behind him, Gemmy was sprawled on the family room floor, and Molly and Martha lay between her front legs and her back legs, using her ample girth as a pillow while they watched a daddy-approved program on television.

While he kept an eye on the clock, anticipating the ring of the doorbell, he opened the file containing the first draft of a research paper he was coauthoring with a colleague.

Kristi had said she would be here at nine, and it was now two minutes past. *Actually, she said* around *nine, and it's not like it matters.* He would be here all day.

The doorbell startled him, even though he'd been expecting it. "I'll be right back," he said to the girls.

He hotfooted it to the front door and opened it to find his mother-in-law standing there.

"Alice. This is a…surprise." And yet another affirmation of why he needed to move.

As always her dark clothing reminded him of a military uniform, and the pinched lines around her mouth made him think she needed to smile once in a while.

"These are the pageant applications. I wasn't sure if you would get around to looking at the website before the deadline." She handed a large envelope to him. "I know how busy you are." Her tone implied otherwise.

He didn't want to get into it with her now, with the girls practically in the next room and Kristi due to arrive any minute. Now he really hoped she got held up somewhere and wouldn't arrive until Alice was gone. "You didn't have to go out of your way. I would have—"

"The girls' photographs are in there with the application forms," Alice said, cutting him off, saving him having to lie to her. "We had them taken the last time Molly and Martha spent the weekend. The applications have to include full-length poses and head shots. We know how busy you are, so we took care of it."

Head shots? He resisted the urge to tear open the envelope.

"I can't stay," she said. "I'm on my way to have my hair done."

Her dark silver coif was as smooth as a helmet, not a hair out of place.

He waved the envelope at her. "I'll take a look at this." *No, you won't, and you shouldn't be letting her think you will.* He needed to put an end to this insanely inappropriate plan to enter his daughters in a beauty pageant.

"Heather would have been okay with this." And without waiting for him to reply, she strode down the sidewalk in her no-nonsense shoes, got into her gray sedan and drove away without a backward glance.

He didn't give a damn what Alice said. Heather would not have been okay with this. What he didn't understand was why this was suddenly so important to Heather's mother.

"Who was that, Daddy?" Molly asked when he returned to the family room.

He slipped the envelope underneath his laptop, glad the girls hadn't heard their grandmother at the door, and even more grateful she hadn't asked to see them.

"Just a courier, sweetie. Dropping off some papers for me to look at."

He sat on a stool and scrolled back to the top of the document and read the introduction for the third time. So much for his plan to get some work done before Kristi arrived.

Who was he kidding? Between Alice's unexpected visit and Kristi's impending arrival, he couldn't concentrate anyway. Last night, after the girls were in bed, he'd spent an hour and a half taking down streamers, cleaning bathrooms and trying to catch up on laundry. Then he'd spent another hour looking at online real estate listings for smaller homes that were still close to the university and the girls' day care, yet a safe distance from his in-laws. His findings weren't impressive. For the first time since deciding to sell this place, he'd had some truly genuine misgivings, but Alice's unexpected visit this morning strengthened his resolve.

The doorbell pealed…this time it had to be Kristi…and on his way to answer it, he reminded himself to play it cool.

"Good morning," she said. In cropped black pants and a pink T-shirt and sneakers, she could be dressed for yoga class. She looked completely different from the woman who had breezed in here yesterday, taken up residence in pretty much every waking thought and occupied at least one of his dreams last night.

Wow. "Good morning." He stood there, realized he was staring at her and hoped he hadn't said "wow" out loud.

"I would have been here sooner, but I waited until my daughter left for school, and then I couldn't find my keys…." She hitched the purple cupcake bag higher on her shoulder. "Sorry. I should have called."

"That's okay. I'm used to students who show up late for class." *Moron.* How was that playing it cool? Had he forgotten how to have a normal conversation with a woman?

She seemed to find him amusing. "Well, I hope I don't lose marks."

She said it with just enough sass to put him in his place, but not so much that he minded.

"Come in," he said, stepping aside for her. This home staging thing was a complete mystery to him but he was more than willing to learn. It would be like being a student again, and he had a pretty good idea he was going to like his teacher.

KRISTI WALKED WITH Nate through the house, noting that the living room doors were open, the streamers were gone and he had even attempted to tame the kitchen clutter.

Molly and Martha were sprawled with the dog in the middle of the family room floor, watching a children's show she didn't recognize. Something new in the years since Jenna was little.

"Good morning, girls. What are you watching?"

Molly angled her head and looked up at her. *"The Cat in the Hat."*

Martha tugged her thumb out of her mouth. *"Knows a Lot About That."* Back went the thumb.

Kristi looked to Nate for an explanation.

"The Cat in the Hat Knows a Lot About That! It's a kids' science show."

Of course it was. This family was all about science. Nate's T-shirt this morning read Evolution of a Botanist and had a series of silhouettes, starting with a chimpanzee, progressing through various human forms, and arriving at a man with a plant pot under one arm. She wondered how many botany T-shirts were among the items of clothing she'd seen lying around his bedroom. She hadn't dared look too closely, but her money was on lots.

The kitchen countertops were still home to more items than potential buyers needed to see, but he'd made a valiant attempt to clear them. She was impressed.

"Coffee?" he asked.

"No, thanks. I've already had tea."

She pulled a file folder and her laptop out of her bag, and carefully set the bag on the floor out of the way. She was not risking a repeat of yesterday's disaster.

She took the stool next to his at the breakfast bar and slid the folder toward him.

"This is my proposal," she said. "I've tried to keep it simple and straightforward. Mostly painting and bringing in some fabrics to freshen things up. I would also like

to give you some solutions to help you keep things organized."

She watched him open the folder and scan the contents,
hoping he wasn't overly offended by her inference that his
home was, well, disorganized.

"Outside, we'll want to uncover the pool, have it cleaned
and filled. It's one of the main selling features of the house.
And…ah…it would be a good idea to turn the pergola back
into a pool house."

Since he was currently using it for his work at the university, she hesitated to suggest that the plants had to go
because she wasn't sure how he would react. She still
didn't really understand exactly what it was that he did.
Last night she had found his page on the university's website, which included a description of his research interests
and a list of papers he'd published recently. She'd hardly
understood a word of it. Who knew plants were so complicated? Or that a man who could pass for a film star would
find them so interesting?

"No problem," he said, surprising her. "Can you give
me a week?"

"Of course. There's lots to do inside."

He closed the folder. "This isn't as bad as I expected.
Where do we start?"

"I've listed the rooms in the order I'd like to work on
them." She had decided to tackle the rooms that were in the
worst shape first. "My plan is to begin with your daughters' bedroom and your office."

"That's fine with me. Is there anything I can do?"

"Yes. If there are items in your office that can be filed
or put in storage, that will help at lot. Those are decisions
I can't make for you."

"Makes sense."

Relieved that he seemed willing to go along with her

suggestions, she pressed on. "This morning I'll get going on the girls' bedroom. I'll bring in some bins they can use to help sort their things."

Nate seemed unsure. "I'm not sure how that'll go over."

Did he think four-year-olds couldn't take ownership of their own messes? she wondered. Or that it was a parent's job to do everything for them?

That could explain why he was so overwhelmed. Or maybe he was overwhelmed and didn't even realize it.

"Let's see how it goes," she said. "I have a couple of tricks up my sleeve."

"Daddy, can we watch something else now?" Molly called from the next room.

"Maybe later. Kristi would like you and Martha to show her your bedroom."

She and Nate slid off their stools and joined the girls in the family room. The TV was already off and both girls were on their feet.

"Come on," Molly said.

Martha took her hand and tugged.

Kristi grabbed her bag and let them lead her down the hallway with Nate following, somewhat reluctantly if she had to guess.

Once inside the room, each girl climbed onto her unmade bed, Kristi sat on an upholstered ottoman, and Nate hovered in the doorway.

"First I'd like to talk about your favorite things," Kristi said.

"Barbie!" Molly said.

Martha shook her head. "Barney!"

Okay, no theme there. "What about colors? What's your favorite?"

"Purple!" they said in unison.

Okay, she could work with that.

"I like purple, too." She pulled a binder and her paint palette out of her bag and fanned the chips to show them. "Is there another color you both like?"

"Blue."

"Red."

Purple, red and blue. Not going to happen. She slid a sample of soft, pale apple green from the palette. "What about this? If we paint your walls pale green, we can use your favorite color as an accent for things like bedding and curtains."

"I yike purple and green," Martha said.

"Me, too."

"I wonder what your dad thinks," Kristi said, glancing at Nate, who was leaning against the door frame.

"Doesn't green clash with purple?"

Kristi flipped the pages in her binder and showed him the color wheel. "They're on opposite sides of the wheel, so they're actually complementary colors." She ran her finger in a line across the page. "Think of a plant that has purple flowers and green leaves."

He leaned in for a closer look. "Okay, that makes sense."

She congratulated herself on the plant analogy. "I suggest a very light shade for the walls, and then we can put together some accessories the girls will enjoy now and that they can take with them. Before we can start painting, we'll need to move all your stuff into the guest room," she said to the girls. "Would you like to help with that?"

Molly bounced on her bed. "Yup. We're good helpers."

Martha stuck her thumb in her mouth and shook her head.

"Why not?" Kristi asked.

"She likes sleeping here," Molly said.

"Martha, is that true?"

The little girl nodded.

Kristi looked to Nate for help.

"I have an idea," he said. "How about we turn this into a little holiday? I'll set up the tent in the family room, and you can sleep in there till your room is ready. It'll be like a camping trip."

Martha's eyes lit up and she gave her head a vigorous nod.

Molly jumped off the bed. "Sleeping bags! Can we have hot dogs? And marshmallows?"

"Sure we can."

Martha leaned close to Kristi and pulled her thumb out of her mouth again. "You, too?" she asked.

Kristi didn't know if she was being invited for hot dogs or the whole camping holiday.

"Thank you for asking me," she said, avoiding looking at Nate. "But I have to go home and have dinner with my daughter."

"She can come."

"How old is she?" Molly sounded as though she was looking for a new playmate.

"She's fourteen. A lot older than you and Martha. She likes hot dogs, though." Camping not so much. "Are you ready to get started?"

Nate stepped into the room. "If we're having hot dogs, we'll have to make a trip to the market. Do you mind if we leave you on your own for a while?"

"I want to stay," Molly said.

Martha's head bobbed in agreement. "I don't yike the market."

"If you don't like the market, I could sure use some help here." Kristi wondered what Nate would think of that. "They'll be fine with me if you'd like to go on your own."

"Are you sure?"

"Of course." She loved kids and these two were adorable. Besides, she had a hunch they would be more willing to cooperate with her cleanup plan if their dad wasn't here.

"Girls, are you okay to stay with Kristi?"

"Yes!" they chorused.

The telephone rang, interrupting their conversation. "I'd better take that," he said.

"While you're still here, I'll bring in the bins I use for sorting."

Kristi followed Nate as far as the foyer. From there he went into the kitchen to get the phone and she let herself out the front door.

Several minutes later she returned with as many plastic bins as she could carry. She set them on the floor inside the front door and went in search of Nate. She hoped he would agree to pare down some of the toys, especially the stuffed animals, but she hadn't wanted to ask in front of the girls.

The dog, still doing a bear-rug imitation, gave her a lazy blink. Nate stood by the patio doors in the family room, his back to her, phone to his ear.

"Mom, I'm sure your friend's daughter is very nice," she heard him say. "And I'd be happy to meet her some other time, but it's Britt's birthday so this should be about her."

He paused to listen to his mother's reply.

Kristi cringed. His mother was obviously trying to set him up with someone, and it was just as clear that he didn't want to be set up. Poor guy. She could relate. Yesterday's call from her mother still echoed in her head, and remembering the story she'd made up brought on a fresh wave of guilt. And she shouldn't be listening to Nate try to wriggle out of a similar situation. This was way too personal.

"Here's the thing," he said. "I'm sort of seeing someone."

Okay, you really need to get out of here, Kristi told herself. But curiosity kept her rooted in the doorway.

"Oh. Ah, her name is Kristi. She's—" He turned around and stopped talking.

Their gazes locked and held.

He ran a hand through his hair. "Mom, I'll call you back. I have to check on the kids." He ended the call without waiting for a response.

The room was suddenly warm and much smaller.

"Oh, God. I am so sorry. I didn't mean for you to hear that." He spiked his hair again. "It's just that my family has this thing about introducing me to women. I was trying to figure a way out of it this time, but I shouldn't have mentioned you."

"A blind date?" Kristi laughed. She couldn't help herself. "Trust me, you do not have to apologize. My family does the same thing to me all the time."

"Really? So…you're not seeing anyone?"

"No, I'm not." Although she was surprised he asked. "A fact that makes my mother a little crazy. Yesterday she called about my aunt's Fourth of July barbecue. She was going to invite this guy who used to live across the street when I was in high school."

"How did you handle it?"

Should she tell him? If she did, it might make him less uncomfortable. "I did the same thing you just did."

His eyes narrowed.

"I told her I'd met someone, and your name kind of slipped out."

There was no humor in his laugh. "So your family thinks you're taking me to your aunt's barbecue."

"I guess so. I'll have to come up with some excuse why you won't be there but—"

"And my mother will expect you to be at the cocktail party she's throwing for my sister's birthday."

She didn't respond, but then he didn't really seem to be talking to her anyway.

"This could work. You come to my sister's birthday party. I go to your aunt's barbecue." He sounded calm and rational, as though he was laying out the steps in a lab experiment. "What do you think?"

She was pretty sure he didn't want to know what she was thinking. "I don't know. I used to lie to my mother about some of the guys I was dating, but I've never lied about someone I'm *not* dating."

He shrugged. "So you'd rather spend an afternoon at a family picnic with the guy who lived across the street?"

God, no. "I'd rather go by myself."

"That's how I feel about my sister's birthday party. But unless I come up with an alternate plan, I'm going to be paired with my mother's bridge partner's daughter."

"So I heard." And she would suffer the same fate if she didn't make plans of her own.

"What is it with families?"

"They mean well," she said. "At least mine does. My mom was a single parent, too, and it was hard for her. I think she always wished she'd find someone but never did, and now she's shifted that focus onto me."

"My family wants to find a new mother for Molly and Martha." His voice was thick with resentment. "They seem to think I'm in over my head."

"Oh, I'm sure they don't. Your girls are great. They're happy. Anyone can see they're well cared for."

"Thank you." The tension around his eyes softened.

"You're welcome."

"So, how about it? You come to my sister's birthday

party, I'll go to your family barbecue, and we'll call it even."

Say no. "Sure," she said instead.

He offered his hand to seal the deal. "It's a date."

She shook it. "A fake date."

"Make that two fake dates." He smiled and her insides turned to Jell-O.

Chapter Four

Kristi tugged her hand out of Nate's and hiked a thumb over one shoulder. "I'll just go and start sorting."

"Sure, good idea. And I'll run out to the market but, ah, first I have to make a call."

Kristi made her escape, collected her things from the foyer and headed down the hallway to the children's bedroom.

He was going to call his mother. There'd be no turning back after that. What were they thinking? What was *she* thinking? Her mother and Aunt Wanda would be happy, but how was she going to explain this to Jenna? Only time would tell if this fake-date idea was brilliant or ill-conceived.

The giggling emanating from Molly and Martha's room was like music to Kristi's ears. Such sweet kids. Each girl was wearing dress-up clothes over their pajamas. Molly's black spaghetti-strap cocktail dress bunched on the floor around her. Martha had a messenger bag slung crosswise over her shoulder and a floppy-brimmed hat all but covered her eyes. Scattered around them were toys and clothes and the largest collection of stuffed animals Kristi had ever seen.

After agreeing to the fake dates, she had completely forgotten that she'd gone into the kitchen to ask Nate about the toys. For now she and the girls would sort them and make decisions later. She looked around for a place to set up the bins and ended up having to clear a space near the door.

"How would you girls like to play a little game?"

"I'm going to a party," Molly said. She twirled, got one foot tangled in the hem of the black dress and collapsed onto a pile of what appeared to be even more dress-up clothes.

Martha giggled. "I'm going on a safari to look for dinosaurs."

"You both look very cute," Kristi said. "Do you like playing dress-up?"

"Yup!" Molly straightened out her dress and bounced to her feet.

"Aunt Britt gave us these clothes," Martha said.

Kristi separated the three bins, set them side by side and took another look around the room. "I need helpers who are good at sorting things."

Martha took off the hat and tossed it in the air. "I can do that. Daddy got us a card game that's all about sorting." The hat landed on one of the beds.

"That sounds like fun." An image of Nate and his daughters playing a card game had Kristi thinking how the world could use more dads like him.

"What are we going to sort?" Molly asked, attempting another twirl, this time successful.

"Let's start with all the clothes on the floor. Do you think you can put your everyday clothes into a red bin and dress-up clothes into the blue one?"

"Yup." Martha pulled the messenger bag over her head and tossed it in the blue bin. "See?"

"Good job."

"I can sort, too." Molly slithered out of the black dress and added it to the blue bin.

"What's going in the yellow bin?" Martha asked.

"Well, let's see…" Kristi pretended to give the question some thought. "I guess some of the stuffed animals could go in there for now. What do you think?"

Molly scooped two teddy bears and a toy killer whale off her bed and dumped them into the yellow bin. Martha followed with a frog, a rabbit and another teddy bear.

"Our grandmas gave us these," Molly said.

"Except for Winnie the Pooh and Curious George. Aunt Britt gave them to us on our birthday."

Kristi recalled the party streamers that Nate must've taken down last night. "Did you have a cake with candles to blow out?"

Both girls shook their heads.

"We had cupcakes!" Martha said.

"Daddy bought them at the store."

"I yike cupcakes better than cake."

Their excitement made Kristi smile. "Me, too."

"Is that why you have them on your purse?"

"It is." She liked that they had noticed her bag. She had found the fabric on sale and had sewn the bag herself. As for birthdays, she made a mental note to suggest to Nate that he ask his family to consider clutter-free gifts, like admission to the Seattle Aquarium or the Children's Museum. It hadn't been easy, but even Kristi's mom had gradually been retrained to give movie passes and iTunes gift cards instead of items Jenna didn't need.

Kristi picked up a purple T-shirt and a pair of jeans. "Who do these belong to?" she asked.

"Me!" Martha reached for them.

"Why are they on the floor?" Kristi asked.

The child shrugged. "There's no room in my dresser."

"Are you sure?" Kristi opened a drawer in one of the matching dressers. Sure enough, it was crammed full.

"Those clothes don't fit us," Molly said.

It took Kristi three tries to get the drawer closed again. No wonder the kids didn't use it. "All right, then. You can put your clothes in the bins for now." Later she would talk to Nate and figure out what to do with the things the girls had outgrown.

Would Nate be open to getting rid of the dressers and building some cubbies for storing the girls' clothes? A couple of months ago Sam had built a modular system for clients who had then taken them to their new home.

"Can you girls keep sorting while I take a look at your dad's office across the hall?"

"Yup."

"We can."

"Good. Maybe there'll even be a prize for the winner." She'd learned long ago that bribery was never a parent's best tactic, but in this case she wasn't the mom. She was just a desperate decorator who wanted all this stuff picked up in the least amount of time.

"What do we win?"

"Well…it just so happens that I brought cupcakes with me. You can each have one at lunchtime, as long as it's okay with your dad."

"Goodie!"

"We yike cupcakes!"

Kristi laughed. "It's a deal, then. I'll come back in a while and see how you're doing."

With the twins engaged in a sorting game, she moved across the hall to the bedroom Nate used as an office. She paused in the doorway, thought of him working here, grading his students' papers, researching the projects she'd read about last night while letting herself indulge in a little daydream about what it would be like to be with a guy like him. Smart, hot, sexy. And now she was about to find out. Not *with him* with him, but spending time with him. A flash of panic caused a flutter in her chest. Fake dating a man she was already attracted to could get complicated.

"Only if you let it." Which she wouldn't. She didn't dare. Besides, she could always change her mind, back out. She knew what that would mean, though. Her high school memory of fending off Bernie Halverson's unwelcome advances flickered through her mind. She wasn't risking a repeat of that. And Nate didn't want a relationship any more than she did, which made this a perfect arrangement. The opposite of complicated.

His office was another story. At one time it must have been a boy's bedroom because two of the walls were papered with sports motifs, the other two were painted bright blue, and the ceiling fixture was a basketball pendant, and a decidedly hideous one at that. How could he work in here?

His large oak desk wasn't old enough to be an antique, but it had that vibe about it. It had been shoved into one corner, and the surface was covered with neat stacks of paper and books, with a clear space in the middle that was about the right size to accommodate the laptop she'd seen on the kitchen peninsula when she arrived a while ago. The floor-to-ceiling shelves that spanned one wall were every bit as crammed as the desk, but like the desk, the books and papers were arranged in neat rows and stacks.

She quickly perused the books on one shelf. Botanical research, plant physiology, forest ecosystems. Molecular phylogenetics, whatever that was. Nate McTavish was one really smart guy, and she couldn't even understand the titles of the books he read. It was a good thing their fake dates would be restricted to family events with plenty of other people around to keep the conversation moving. If they went on an actual date, just the two of them, they would never find anything to talk about.

Here in his office she saw the same kind of organization she'd noticed in the greenhouse yesterday. He had a ton of stuff but she was willing to bet he had a system, that he knew exactly where to look if he needed something. If she had to describe her idea of what a scientist's brain looked like, this would be it. Lots and lots of neat compartments overflowing with information but at the same time never quite full.

She knew better than to try to organize this room, although it would be nice if Nate would agree to reduce some of the sheer volume of it, maybe store the things he didn't need in boxes. Until the house was sold, she would like to create a better sense of space here. Would Nate be as eager to tackle his office as the two little girls chattering in their room across the hall? Maybe he liked cupcakes, too. That made her smile.

She would also swing the desk around and away from the wall to give it the importance it deserved, and so he didn't sit with his back to the door. She wouldn't tell him its present position was bad feng shui—he'd probably think that was totally unscientific—but when she was finished in here, she knew he'd find it a more productive place to work.

She pulled her notebook out of her bag. At the top of a clean page she jotted "Nate's Office" and started a list. She was still making notes when her BlackBerry buzzed a few minutes later. The Ready Set Sold office number appeared on the screen. Their morning conference call. Claire was right on time, as always. This would give her and Sam a chance to discuss her ideas for Nate's place. As for other developments with this client, well, she might hold off talking about those.

AFTER NATE WAS sure that Kristi was down the hall and out of earshot, he dialed his mother's number before he lost his nerve. While it rang, he let himself out through the patio doors and walked to his greenhouse, where there was no chance of being overheard. His mother would be full of questions and in case he needed to get creative, he'd rather Kristi not have a chance to eavesdrop.

"Hi, Mom," he said when she answered. "Sorry I had to cut you off."

"No problem. Are the girls okay?"

"Oh, yeah. They were just…ah…being a little too quiet so I thought I'd better check on them."

"Of course. So, about Friday night. Your father and I are throwing a little cocktail party to celebrate Britt's thirtieth. I wanted to give you enough notice so you can find a sitter for the girls. And of course now we're hoping your *friend* can join us."

He drew a deep breath and took the plunge. "I just talked to her and she's free. So yes, we'll be there."

"Wonderful. You said her name is Kristi? We can't wait to meet her. I'm glad we talked before I invited Evelyn's daughter."

So was he. "So, about the party. Do I…*we*…do we need to bring a gift?" He hated shopping for anything, groceries included, but he could always grab some flowers on his way there.

"It would be a brave man who showed up empty-handed at Britt's birthday party."

Flowers it is.

"We're also having a family brunch on Sunday and of course you'll bring the girls for that. Kristi, too."

The fake date tally rose to three. And he would have to take another gift, and it couldn't be flowers. "We'll be there."

Would Kristi agree to go? He hoped so. He had no more interest in meeting Evelyn's daughter than he'd had any of the other daughters, sisters and second cousins twice removed of his mother's friends. In the past six months she and his sister had introduced him to a string of women deemed to be suitable wife-and-mother material. Apparently they discussed his sorry existence with everyone they knew. He shuddered to think how those conversations played out, but he could well imagine they'd read like an ad on an online dating site.

Desperate widower seeks equally desperate single woman. Must love kids and dogs.

Not anymore. He and Kristi had an arrangement that was both mutually beneficial and blissfully uncomplicated.

"I should go, Mom. I'll see you on Friday."

"Tell Kristi we're looking forward to meeting her."

"She's looking forward to meeting you and Dad, too," he added because he knew that's what she wanted to hear.

"See you on Friday. And Nate, we're so glad you're seeing someone. All any of us want is for you to be happy."

Leaving him alone would make him happy. Taking Kristi to his sister's birthday party would feel a lot like being under a microscope, but it couldn't be as bad as any of the blind dates he had agreed to. Like the one he'd met for coffee and an awkward conversation after work last month. Or the woman he and the girls had met at the park one Saturday afternoon when the babysitter backed out at the last moment. That woman had made a valiant effort to find his daughters engaging, and failed dismally.

Back in the kitchen, he dropped the phone into its cradle and scrawled the time and dates of his sister's two birthday parties on the magnetic calendar on the fridge door. Before he left for the market he should do a little tidying up in the kitchen. He stowed the girls' breakfast dishes and his coffee mug in the dishwasher and wiped down the counter. He closed his laptop and lifted it up, uncovering the pageant information Alice had dropped off. Kristi's arrival and his mother's phone call had pushed all this nonsense out of his mind. He set his computer down, picked up the envelope and removed the contents. Fanning through the pages, he saw there were application forms, which Alice had conveniently completed, waivers that required his signature, a bio for each girl, and pages of information about the venue and answers to frequently asked questions. Alice had clipped a note to the sheets describing the contestants' talent, pointing out that if the girls were taking ballet or piano lessons, they could also enter this part of the pageant. The head shots were at the bottom of the stack.

Nate set the application package on the counter and stared at the photographs. Molly and Martha stared back. Instead of their usual pigtails, which were the only way he knew to manage their flyaway blond curls, they each had a poufy updo with flower barrettes that matched clothes he'd never seen before. He took a closer look. Was that makeup? Had Alice actually put makeup on his kids, got them dolled up and taken them to a photographer? How did he not know about this? He remembered them saying they'd had pictures taken, but he assumed Alice and Fred had done them. Dammit, what was this woman thinking? This crossed a line.

He stuffed everything back in the envelope, fighting the urge to toss it in the fireplace with a match and a can of kerosene. That would be the easy way to resolve this. What he needed to do, what he should have done long ago, was sit down with Alice and Fred and remind them who called the shots here. He did. He was Molly and Martha's father, he made the decisions and they needed to back off. Way the hell off.

He tucked the laptop and the envelope under his arm and strode through the house. For now he would put this stuff away and deal with his in-laws when he cooled off a little and wouldn't say anything he'd regret. Then he would find Kristi and break the news that two fakes had turned into three, an idea that was sounding better by the minute.

"GOOD MORNING, CLAIRE." Kristi settled into Nate's creaky old desk chair with her BlackBerry in her hand and her notebook on her lap.

"Hi, Kristi. Sam's on the line, too."

"Hey, Sam. How's it going?"

"Good. I'm finishing up at the Baxter house this morning."

"That's the place that needed the faux wood paneling stripped out of the living room?"

"That's the one. And I'm happy to say the drywall underneath was in good shape, except for the nail holes. It's been patched and primed, and I'm painting it this morning."

"Big job." Claire, who claimed she didn't know one end of a hammer from the other, was always impressed by Sam's work.

"The paneling was a lot easier to take down than wallpaper," Sam said.

Kristi took that as an opportunity to shift the conversation to Nate's place. "I was just thinking about you and wallpaper. I need some stripped from one of the bedrooms here in the McTavish house."

Sam groaned.

"Just two walls."

"That's it?"

"That's it. I promise."

"You're sure you can't make it work?"

"Not a chance, and when you see it, I think you'll agree." The juxtaposition of the sports motifs with Nate's old desk and scholarly-looking books was laughable. "It was a boy's bedroom at one time, but the current owner uses it as an office."

"Speaking of the owner…" Claire said.

Here we go. "What about him?"

"He's very photogenic," Sam said.

Kristi doodled in the margin of her notebook. "He is, isn't he?"

Sam, usually so serious, was laughing. "You've photographed a lot of homes, but I've never seen you take pictures of the owners. Last night you sent three of this guy."

"And we thank you for it." Even Claire thought it was funny.

"I sent photographs of the house—he just happened to be in them." That wasn't exactly true, not even a little bit, especially considering how much time she'd spent looking at them.

Should she tell them about the latest development? She had more or less decided not to, but if she didn't tell someone, she was going to explode.

"He seems nice," she said, keeping her voice low. "He invited me to a party on Friday night."

Several long seconds ticked by before Sam or Claire said anything, and then they were both talking at once.

"That was fast."

"You already have a date with him?"

"How did that happen?"

"Are you sure this is a good idea, hon?"

No, she wasn't sure of anything, including her spurof-the-moment decision to tell Sam and Claire. "It's not a date," she said. "Not a real one."

"If it's not a 'real' date, what kind of date is it?" Sam asked.

"It's sort of a fake date." Except it had sounded okay when she'd said it in her head. Out loud it sounded ridiculous. She could hardly blame them for laughing. "It's really just one of those crazy coincidences. You know what my mother's like. She wanted to set me up with a date for my aunt's Fourth of July barbecue, and Nate's family tried to arrange a date for him to take to his sister's birthday party. So we're going together. We're not interested in *dating* dating, so this is a perfect arrangement. Neither of us has to suffer another blind date, and our families back off with their matchmaking."

"So you're going on two fake dates, and both will be spent with your families?"

"Our families are the reason we're doing this. If we went out, just the two of us, then it would be a real date. That's not going to happen."

"Isn't this going to get complicated?" The ever-practical Claire never took risks.

To Kristi, being at her aunt's barbecue with Bernie Halverson was complicated. Especially if he tried to kiss her. Just the idea of it made Kristi shudder. Nate wasn't likely to kiss a woman he wasn't dating, and she probably wouldn't mind if he did.

"What are you going to tell Jenna?"

She'd been wondering the same thing. She still had to set an example for her daughter, after all. "I'll downplay the whole thing, make sure she understands we're just friends."

"I hope you have fun," Claire said. "You deserve it. I'm

sorry if I didn't sound supportive at first, but you caught me by surprise."

"And we don't want to see you get hurt," Sam said. "I'm sure it's nice to meet another single parent, though. You both already have a lot in common."

"Not really. For one thing he's smart, and I mean *really* smart."

"And hot," Sam said.

Claire laughed. "Hot and smart. Two more things he has in common with our Kristi."

"I wish. He's not just average, everyday smart. He's university-professor smart. He studies all kinds of scientific things about plants and hybrids. You should see the books he reads. I don't even know what some of the titles mean. And then there are Greek gods, Roman gods. He's a walking encyclopedia."

"What do Greek and Roman gods have to do with hybridized plants?" Claire asked.

"Nothing. We were talking about our dogs' names."

"S-o-o-o…" Sam drew out the word for effect. "Let's get this straight. He's single, he's smart, he's hot, he obviously must love dogs, but all you want is a fake date."

"I said yes to the date because there are no strings attached. You know me well enough to realize there's no way I'll take a chance on another deadbeat."

Kristi heard the groans and knew rolling eyes accompanied them.

Claire spoke first. "Sweetie, you said it yourself. He's smart. And last time I checked, university professor is not exactly a deadbeat occupation."

"And he's hot," Sam said.

"You know what I mean."

"We do," Claire said. "You're a wonderful mom, an amazing woman—"

"Who deserves to have a hot guy in her life," Sam said.

"Enough! The two of you sound like my mother." Except that her mother had yet to come up with anyone who qualified as hot. "I should get back to work. I'll see you at our next meeting. Nine o'clock, right?"

"That's right," Claire said. "At the usual place."

"It's in my calendar. I'll see you both then." Kristi tucked her BlackBerry into her bag and tried to refocus on the lists she'd been working on before taking the call. What was the point? She closed the book and shoved it in her bag. She needed to check on Molly and Martha anyway. It was her job to keep an eye on them till their father was back from the market.

NATE PARKED HIS SUV in the driveway, got out and carried two bags of groceries through the breezeway and the side door that led to the mudroom and kitchen. A couple of hours ago he'd congratulated himself on having his personal life firmly back in his control, but all the way to the market and back he'd pondered the newsflash that, according to Kristi, he was a *deadbeat*.

Seriously? He'd wanted to let her know that his mother was throwing two parties this weekend instead of just one. He didn't want to talk about it in front of the girls, so he'd planned to invite her to join him in the kitchen.

Molly and Martha's chatter had drifted past the door, which was slightly ajar. Luckily they hadn't seen him. He had heard Kristi's voice, too, but she hadn't been in the girls' room. She was in his office across the hall, sitting there in his chair with her back to the door and her phone to her ear.

She said something about no strings attached, and then she'd said, "You know me well enough to realize there's no way I'll take a chance on another deadbeat."

She had paused, listening to what the other person had to say. He had hightailed it back to the kitchen, not wanting to hear any more.

Kristi had agreed to go out with him because there were no strings attached. Fair enough. They were both on the same page. But did she really think he was a deadbeat? Had he completely misinterpreted all the signs?

As he put the groceries away he debated what to do. He supposed he should let Kristi and the girls know he was back, but he was in no hurry to face her. Instead he poured himself a cup of coffee and stared out the kitchen window. He still had to break the news that there were two parties this weekend instead of one, and by now his mother would have told Britt he was bringing a date. Hell, she'd probably sent out a press release.

Maybe you're looking at this from the wrong perspective, he told himself. Kristi had agreed to pose as his date at his sister's birthday party if he would reciprocate and attend her aunt's barbecue. No strings attached. That's what she'd said; that's what they both wanted. If going together to these functions meant no blind dates, no unexpected setups with strangers, did it really matter what she thought of him? Not one bit, he decided. She wasn't perfect, either. Not that he'd seen any major flaws yet, but she was bound to have at least one.

"Daddy, come see our room."

He swung around, expecting to see Molly. Instead he got an eyeful of Kristi, holding Martha's hand on one side and Molly's on the other. They were all smiling at him.

He mustered a smile in return and set his coffee cup on the counter. "Let's take a look."

He joined them, avoiding eye contact with Kristi. Both girls seemed content to hold her hands, so he was left to follow them down the hall. They stopped outside the bedroom door, Molly and Martha grinning impishly. He humored them by being the first to go inside, prepared to feign surprise, and being thoroughly taken aback when he saw what they had accomplished.

"Wow. Great job, girls." And he meant it. Except for the furniture and Kristi's big, brightly colored plastic bins, the floor that had been obscured by his daughters' belongings was now clear.

"We had a race," Martha said, her eyes like miniature saucers, as though even she couldn't quite believe what they'd done.

"We put dress-up clothes in the blue boxes and our clothes in the red boxes," Molly said.

"And stuffies in the yellow boxes," Martha tried unsuccessfully to push the overflow of stuffed animals beneath the rim. "Just like Kristi told us."

"Who won the race?" he asked.

"We both did. Kristi said."

He finally allowed himself to make eye contact with the woman who had accomplished more in half an hour, by simply turning work into a game, than he could have managed in a whole week of cajoling. "Thank you."

Her smile, so genuine, made it hard to believe she was the same woman who had called him a deadbeat earlier that morning.

"You're welcome. They're good workers. I might have to hire them as my assistants." She tweaked their pigtails, and they both giggled. "And now they each get a cupcake at lunchtime, as long as that's okay with you. I have some out in my van."

"Sure. I got everything I need to make hot dogs, too." And since she had offered dessert, it would be rude not to include her. "You're welcome to join us."

"Yay! Hot dogs!"

"Yay! Cupcakes!"

"We found our coloring books." Molly pointed to their little table. "I'm going to color."

"Me, too." Martha settled onto one of the chairs.

"I'd like to talk to your dad about his office," Kristi said.

The girls, already intent on choosing crayons, didn't respond.

She slipped out of the room and he followed her across the hall.

"That's pretty amazing," he said. "What you got them to do in there."

"I think they had fun." She consulted several lists on a page in her notebook. "I have some suggestions to help you streamline the things in their room, but first I'd like to go over my ideas for your office."

He would like to go over her idea that he was a deadbeat, but bringing it up now didn't feel right, and he wasn't ready to hear what she had to say anyway. Instead he listened as she outlined her plan, and then indicated the bundle of flattened boxes that he could assemble and use to sort and store papers. She showed him the paint color she had in mind, and he agreed it would be an improvement over the blue. He had never liked it anyway. And he was fine to get rid of the wallpaper.

She pulled a small pocket knife from her bag—was there anything she didn't have in there? he wondered—and cut the strap on the bundle of boxes. "We might as well assemble these while we talk."

That was fine with him. He watched her turn one of the neatly folded pieces into a box with a lid, and followed her lead.

"If you're okay with the colors, I'll order the paint this afternoon. For the master bedroom, I'd like to use a similar green but a few shades darker. It'll be a little more dramatic. The off-white in the fourth bedroom is nice and neutral so I'll leave it and bring in some green accessories to tie everything together."

"It all sounds good."

"I have a meeting with my business partners first thing tomorrow morning. After that our carpenter will drop by and measure for the new bookshelves in here. I have some ideas for organizing your daughters' room, too."

Between them they had assembled five boxes and she was still folding.

"I was also wondering how you feel about putting some of their things in storage. After the house is listed and being shown, I think it'll be easier for you…and them… if there's less stuff for you to manage."

He had only thought of moving as a way to get distance from his in-laws, but now he could see that streamlining their belongings would really streamline their lives. Across the hall, Molly and Martha sat happily coloring at a table that had always been buried beneath clutter. How had he let that happen?

"Putting things in storage is a good idea. My sister keeps giving them dress-up clothes, and some of their own clothes are getting too small. And every time they see their grandparents, we add two more stuffed animals to the zoo."

She smiled. "Could you ask them to hold off on that for now? At least until you've moved?"

"Of course." He should have asked them to stop a long time ago.

"For things that don't fit anymore, I know a great consignment store that takes good-quality children's clothes, and I can also arrange to donate things to charity."

"You don't mind doing that?" He wished he could stay

annoyed with her, but she was so patient, and so helpful, and she smelled so damned good.

"I don't mind at all. It's actually part of my job."

"Well, I still appreciate it." And in spite of what she thought of him, he was glad she was willing to go to his sister's party weekend. "I talked to my mother again, and there's one minor change in plans."

"Oh? What's that?"

"There's a family brunch on Sunday. I hope you don't mind going to that, too. I didn't know how to say no."

Instead of being annoyed, she laughed. "If they're anything like my family, saying no isn't easy."

"So you don't mind?"

She added another box to the pile. "Is your mom a good cook?"

"She's a great cook."

"Then I don't mind at all." Instead of looking at him, she pulled a black marker from her bag and handed it to him. "This should be enough boxes to get you started, and you can use this to label them. I also brought in a blue bin for recycling. I'll let you get started while I go order the paint. And then, if you'd like, I'll help you make lunch."

"I'd like that." She was being so nice. Had he misunderstood what she'd said on the phone? Did it matter? She had also said "no strings attached." No matter how nice she was and how great she smelled, she was absolutely right, and he'd better not let himself forget it.

Chapter Five

After dinner on Friday, Nate cleaned up the kitchen, got the girls ready for bed and settled down at the kitchen counter with his computer. After putting in a full day working on his house, Kristi had gone home with a promise to be back in two hours. Those two hours were nearly up, and they felt more like four. Under normal circumstances he would have picked her up. He hadn't been able to find a sitter, though, so she had volunteered her teenage daughter. It made sense that she would drop Jenna off and they would leave from here.

From where he sat, he could see Molly and Martha in their pajamas, curled up with Gemmy in front of the TV in the family room. It wasn't a show they normally watched, but it seemed harmless enough.

He leaped to his feet when the doorbell pealed. The girls jumped up, too, Gemmy heaved herself onto all fours, and they followed him to the front door.

Kristi, all smiles, was worth the wait. He had pictured her wearing a little black dress but realized he would have been disappointed if she had. Her green cocktail dress was almost a perfect match for her eyes. With a fitted waist, a modest halter-style neckline and a skirt that flared softly to her knees, she looked a lot curvier than she did in yoga pants and a T-shirt. She'd let her hair down and he liked it. A lot.

Beside her stood a younger version of her. Jenna was wearing black leggings or tights or whatever kids called them, and over them she had on a pair of tattered denim cutoffs with the bottoms rolled up. Her baggy black-and-white-striped pullover had long sleeves and frayed cuffs with thumb holes cut in them. Her hair was shaggier and a few shades lighter than her mother's, and her eye makeup a lot thicker and darker. He knew nothing about fashion trends, but grunge came to mind. Kristi had said she was fourteen, and he supposed this was what he had to look forward to in ten years.

"Hi, Nate. Hi, girls. This is my daughter, Jenna. Jenna, this is Nate and his daughters."

"I'm Molly. She's Martha."

Nate tried to ease Martha's thumb out of her mouth so she could speak for herself. She was having none of it.

"Hi," Jenna said. She even had her mother's smile. "It must be cool being twins. I always wanted a sister."

"I'm the oldest," Molly said.

Martha nodded, clinging to his leg with one arm.

"This is Gemmy. She's our dog."

Martha released her thumb long enough to say, "I want a kitten."

Jenna scratched Gemmy's head. "She's huge. I brought my dog, too." She shot Nate a quick look. "My mom said it was okay."

He nodded.

"Would you like to meet him?" she asked his daughters.

"Where is he?" Molly asked.

"He's in here," Kristi said, patting what could pass for a woman's handbag. "Thanks for letting us bring him. He's okay at home during the daytime when I'm at work and Jenna's at school, but he doesn't like to be left alone at night."

"No problem. Gemmy's good with other dogs."

Jenna closed the door, and Kristi set the bag on the floor and unzipped it. A small, shaggy head emerged, followed by what just might be the scrawniest excuse for a dog Nate had ever seen. And it was wearing clothes. He fought a brief battle with his arching eyebrows, and lost.

Martha let go of his leg and crouched on the floor. "Look, Gemmy. A puppy."

The poor little thing started to shiver.

Jenna knelt next to Martha and picked up the little dog. "He's not a puppy. This is as big as he'll get."

"He's wearing a sweater," Molly said.

"It's a polo shirt," Jenna said.

"I yike him." Martha gently stroked the top of his head. "Daddy, can we get a dog yike this?"

"You just said you want a kitten." Not that he had any intention of getting one. Or another dog for that matter, not even a rat-size one.

"Daddy, can we get clothes for Gemmy?" Molly asked.

"Dogs don't—" He cut himself off before he blurted out that dogs don't need clothes. "Dogs like Gemmy have lots of fur to keep them warm. If she needs a shirt, I guess she can wear one of mine."

The twins giggled.

Gemmy, who had been staring at the newcomer as though not sure what to make of him, took a step closer, lowered her snout and gave him a sniff. Nate grabbed a towel off the closet doorknob and wiped the drool from her jowls.

Kristi watched the dogs' tentative nose-to-nose greeting, then smiled up at him. "It'll take Hercules a while to get used to a new dog and different surroundings. Jenna can keep him in the carrier."

The Yorkie let out a single sharp bark.

Gemmy's ears perked up and she backed away. Nate laughed at the Saint's reaction to the yipping, quivering Yorkie, who didn't amount to much more than a large dust bunny. He grasped her collar and tugged.

"Come on in," he said to Jenna. "I'll show you where everything is and give you a rundown of the girls' routine."

They all trooped into the family room.

"You have a tent in here," Jenna said to the twins. "Cool."

"That's where we sleep."

"'Cause your mom took everything out of our room."

Kristi tweaked their pigtails. "Just until it's painted. Then you can move back in."

"Green," the girls chorused.

Molly held up the flap. "Come in and see. We got sleeping bags."

"And pillows and teddy bears."

"You can sleep here, too, if you want."

Jenna thanked them and admired the interior of the tent, agreeing that it looked very cozy.

With the girls and Gemmy settled in the family room and Kristi chatting with them about Hercules and asking about the television show they were watching, he showed Jenna the list of numbers he'd made for her. His cell phone, his parents' home phone number, Britt's cell number. He had briefly considered adding his in-laws, but decided not to. Not that he anticipated an emergency, but if something came up, he didn't want to explain why he hadn't asked them to look after the girls, and why he had a date with his interior decorator.

Jenna pulled a cell phone from her pocket. "I'll put the numbers in here. I have my mom's, too."

He watched Kristi's daughter carefully program the contacts into her phone. "There," she said. "If anything comes up, I just have to push a button."

Kristi got up off the sofa and joined them. "Ready to go?"

Jenna studied him like an amoeba under a microscope, then shifted her examination to her mother. "This is so weird."

"What is?"

"You…going on a date."

"It's not a date," he and Kristi said in perfect unison, their gazes locking briefly before they both looked away.

Jenna rolled her eyes. "Yeah, I know. You're just friends. Yada, yada. And it only took you an hour to get ready."

Kristi flushed. He understood why she'd be embarrassed, but it was an hour well spent. Kristi looked beautiful with her glossy blond hair curling in loose waves around her shoulders, the stunning green dress hugging her body and showing off those amazing legs. Until now he hadn't noticed her shoes, strappy white heels that matched the small white handbag she was carrying and the shawl draped over her arm. He was glad she hadn't changed perfumes. This one was so her, and he liked it.

His family would approve of her, too, as long as they didn't find out they were being duped. He needed to make sure that didn't happen, but for tonight, he was actually looking forward to being in the company of a woman—a very beautiful woman—who was no more interested in being in a relationship than he was. He could even overlook the fact that she thought he was a deadbeat.

"Where are you going, Daddy?"

"To your aunt Britt's b—" Geez, he'd almost blurted out *birthday party*. He'd never hear the end of it.

Jenna saved him. "They're going to some boring grown-up thing." She held up a bag. "I brought a DVD for us to watch—*The Parent Trap*—it's about twins. And some books I thought you might like, and some microwave popcorn. I hope that's okay?"

Molly grabbed for the bag and even Martha let go of her thumb. "We yike popcorn!"

"Popcorn is fine," he said. "Just be sure to brush your teeth before bed, okay?"

Molly climbed onto a stool at the counter, chattering nonstop while Jenna pressed buttons on the microwave. Martha curled up on the sofa with Hercules, who had retreated into his carrier.

"Good night." He planted a kiss on top of Molly's head.

"G'night, Daddy. We're making the popcorn right now so we can eat it as soon as the movie starts."

"Good idea." He lowered himself to the sofa and gave one of Martha's pigtails a gentle tug. "Good night."

She was peering through the mesh window of the pet carrier. "Can we get a dog yike Herca— Herca—"

"Hercules." It was good to see Martha with both hands occupied and her thumb out of her mouth for a change.

"Except I wanna girl dog with a purple dress."

Oh, geez. "I have to go, sweetie. Kristi and I don't want to be late. We'll talk about this later, okay?"

They did not need another dog. Or more laundry. "Good night, girls. Have fun and be good for Jenna," he said. "For tonight, it's okay for them to stay up till the movie's over." They'd most likely be asleep before then anyway.

"Yay!" the twins chimed.

"Have fun on your 'this-is-not-a-date' date." She gave her mother a saucy little wink.

"Teenagers," Kristi said, walking with him to the front door. "See what you have to look forward to?"

"Times two." He hadn't spent any time around teenage girls since he'd been a teenager, and that didn't count. "She seems very grown-up. How old did you say she is?"

"Fourteen. Most days. She still has moments when she acts like a ten-year-old but the rest of the time she's fourteen going on twenty-one."

He reached for the doorknob and hesitated, glancing back to the family room for one last look.

"She's great with little kids. You don't have anything to worry about."

"Good to know." He picked up a bouquet of flowers off the table in the foyer. "For my sister," he explained.

"Ooo, those are pretty. Do you think I should have brought something for her?"

"Not at all. These will be from both of us."

He held the door open for her, followed her out and locked up behind them.

"If you like, we can take my van."

"I thought we'd take my old Beetle. I don't get to drive it very often because it doesn't have anchors for the girls' car seats, but it could use a run. Do you mind?"

"Not at all. Jenna was really excited when she saw it in your driveway. She said it's the kind of car she wants to buy when she's old enough to get her license. I didn't want to burst her bubble by telling her there's no way we can afford another car."

He opened the passenger door for her. "It's a nice night. We can even put the top down if you don't mind a little wind in your hair."

"Ordinarily I would say top down for sure, but since we're going to a party and I'll be meeting your family, I should probably arrive looking presentable."

"Good point." He circled to the driver's side and got in, thinking it would take more than a little breeze to ruin her appearance.

"It is a cute car. How long have you had it?"

He started the engine. "Since I graduated from high school. My aunt bought a new car, couldn't get much for this in a trade-in, so she passed it on to me."

"That was lucky."

He backed out of the driveway. "I didn't think so at the time. I had my eye on a Pontiac Firebird."

Kristi gave him a long look. "I'm having a hard time picturing a university professor and a dad driving a car like that."

"I did mention that I had just graduated from high school, didn't I? I wasn't looking for safe or sensible or economical."

"Let me guess. You thought a Firebird would be a chick magnet."

"Yeah, well, in the head of a teenage boy, it doesn't sound so tacky."

"Oh, I know how it is for teenage boys."

It was his turn to look at her. "You know someone who has one?"

She looked away. "I did. Jenna's dad."

Okay. He hadn't thought about it until now, but Kristi couldn't be much over thirty and her daughter was fourteen. That meant she was just a teenager herself when she became a parent. For some reason, that got him thinking about the condom she'd had in her bag the day they met. He shouldn't put condoms and Kristi into the same thought. Still, he gave the little white purse on her lap a quick glance, and for one fleeting moment he wondered what was in it.

NATE'S PARENTS LIVED in a stately two-story brick house, built in the forties, Kristi guessed, on a spacious lot with a sweeping front drive. The lawn was immaculate, the shrubs sculpted and the flower beds carefully tended.

"What a lovely home," she said as Nate pulled up and parked. "And such a gorgeous garden."

"All thanks to my mother. She's the green thumb in the family."

"So that's where you get your interest in plants?"

"I'm afraid not. I started university with the idea of becoming a veterinarian, but the botany component of one of my biology courses changed all of that. I'm interested in the science of plants, though. That doesn't necessarily translate to the garden."

Considering the state of Nate's yard, that explained a lot.

"Wait here," Nate said. He stepped out of the car and quickly came around to open her door. He took the flowers she was holding and extended a hand to help her out.

She didn't mind opening doors for herself, but it was nice to be given some special treatment every now and then. Even nicer that he was such a gentleman, and that he seemed to do these little things without thinking about them.

She teetered slightly when her heels hit the pavement, making her regret she'd opted for these shoes instead of the flats. Nate held her hand till she regained her balance, then she looked into his eyes and nearly lost her composure.

"Ready?" he asked.

Not even a little bit.

He held her hand all the way up to the front door, probably in case someone was watching from inside, she told herself. With that thought, her nerves nearly got the best of her. She was going to meet his family, a family who thought she and Nate were dating, maybe even believed there was more to their relationship than that.

"I just have one question before we go in," she said.

"What's that?"

"How well do your parents think we know each other?"

He grinned down at her. "I don't know. Whatever they think, they didn't hear it from me."

"I didn't mean *that*. I just wondered if you told them how long we've been seeing each other. *Supposedly* seeing each other."

"I didn't say."

"What if someone asks? What if they want to know how we met?" She hadn't thought of that until now. "What do we tell them?"

"Why don't we go with the truth? I hired your company to sell my house, the two of us hit it off. Easier to keep our stories straight that way."

He was right, of course. No sense making this more complicated than it needed to be. "That's a good idea."

He squeezed her hand. "My mother actually throws a pretty good party. Let's just relax and enjoy ourselves." And then he opened the front door without ringing the bell and led her inside.

The entryway was small but elegantly decorated with a mosaic tile floor, a walnut console table and an antique mirror flanked by wall sconces. Kristi hardly had a chance to take in her surroundings before a petite brunette in a formfitting, retro-inspired red wiggle dress threw her arms around Nate's neck. It was a stunning dress, one Kristi was sure she could never afford, but definitely something she could replicate on her sewing machine.

"You're here! Oh, are these flowers for me? They're beautiful!"

Nate hugged her back and relinquished the flowers.

"Happy birthday, sis. I hope you weren't expecting anything extravagant."

"From you?" she asked, laughing. "Never. Hi, you must be Kristi. I'm Nate's sister, Britt. The birthday girl. Happy to finally meet you. I've heard *so* much about you."

Kristi shot Nate a look. "You have?"

He took her hand, squeezed it again reassuringly. "Don't listen to her. She's just messing with me."

"I am," she said, a hint of mischief in her blue eyes. "He's been keeping us in the dark about you. That's brothers for you, but now that you're here I can't wait to get to know you. Come on, I'll introduce you to our parents." She passed the flowers back to Nate. "Be a sweetie and take these into the kitchen for me? And get Kristi something to drink. What would you like? A martini? Cosmopolitan? Wine? There's also mineral water if you prefer something nonalcoholic."

Feeling a little breathless just listening to her, Kristi glanced over her shoulder at Nate as his sister hurried her toward the sound of conversation and laughter in the living room. "A glass of white wine would be nice."

"I'll catch up with you." He disappeared, leaving Kristi to fend for herself.

"Mom!" Britt was waving across the sea of people who filled the living room. "Nate and Kristi are here."

They wound their way between groups of people and met in the middle of the room.

"Mom, this is Nate's girlfriend. Kristi, my mom, Helen McTavish."

Kristi extended her hand and found herself in a warm embrace instead.

"Hello, dear. We've been looking forward to meeting you." Helen McTavish had passed along her short stature to her daughter, and her captivating smile and blue, blue eyes to both of her children. She wore an expensive-looking navy pantsuit with a coral blouse that complemented her coloring. "What a beautiful dress you're wearing. That color is perfect for you."

"Oh, thank you."

"I love it, too," Britt said. "Where did you get it?"

"I made it myself, actually."

"You sewed that?" Britt eyed her dress with renewed interest. "Okay, now I am seriously impressed, and more than a little jealous."

Hoping this was a sign she was making a good impression, Kristi decided not to tell them she'd whipped it up last night after going through her closet and deciding none of her options were quite right for this occasion.

The doorbell chimed. "I'll get that," Britt said. "Be right back."

"You're very talented," Helen said. "That son of mine has excellent taste."

Flustered by the attention, Kristi decided it was time to change the subject. "I was admiring your front garden when we arrived. Nate tells me you're an avid gardener."

"How sweet of you to notice."

Before she could respond, Nate appeared at her side with a glass in each hand. He gave her the white wine she'd requested, then slid that hand around her waist as casually as if he'd done it a dozen times. Then he touched the rim of his beer glass to her wine goblet.

"I see you've met my mother."

Helen offered her cheek and he bent down and gave it a kiss.

"You look beautiful, Mom."

"Thank you, dear. Kristi was telling me how much she likes our front yard." Helen was still beaming. "Are you a gardener, too?" she asked.

"I try to grow a few things in planters on my patio, but I'm afraid I don't know much about plants."

"That's okay. Neither does Nate." She laughed at her own joke.

"Very funny, Mom." But Nate was laughing, too. "Did Kristi mention that I showed her my greenhouse?" He pulled her even closer as he said it and she went willingly, taking a nervous sip of her drink as she did.

Helen wagged a finger at him. "You be careful, young man. I wasn't born yesterday and I know a smart aleck when I see one."

"Yes, ma'am."

"Kristi said she sewed this dress herself," Helen said. "You told me she was beautiful but you didn't mention she was so talented, as well."

"What was I thinking?"

Kristi couldn't bring herself to look at him, and she was pretty sure he would avoid eye contact anyway.

Britt rejoined them. "So, how did the two of you meet?" she asked. "I don't think you mentioned that, either."

He smiled down at her then with an I-told-you-so sparkle in his eyes. "Remember I told you I hired a real estate company to help me sell the house?"

"Yes, although I'm still surprised you want to sell," Britt said. "I've always thought that was a perfect house for you and...you and the girls."

"Kristi is one of the owners of that company," Nate responded without missing a beat.

"Are you now?" Helen studied her with even more interest. "So you're a real estate agent?"

"No, I'm an interior decorator. One of my business partners is a Realtor, though, and the other is a carpenter. Our company is called Ready Set Sold. We help our clients renovate and stage their homes before they go on the market."

"I'm impressed. And since you're helping Nate get the house ready to sell, I take it you've already met my two darling granddaughters and that behemoth of a dog of theirs."

"I have. The girls are adorable." They were, and in just a few short days she had grown far more attached to them than common sense dictated. "And Gemmy is…" She had no idea what a behemoth was, but she guessed it was large. "Gemmy is the biggest dog I've ever met, especially compared to mine, who happens to be one of the smallest you'll ever see."

"So you love dogs and you're good with children. You're artistic and entrepreneurial. No wonder Nate is so taken with you."

He looked down at her, and during those few brief seconds while their gazes locked, all of this…Nate's affection, Britt's admiration, Helen's approval…it didn't just feel real. She wanted it to be real.

"Britt, why don't you and Nate go out to the backyard and see if you can find your father? And make sure Ned Grainger from next door didn't give him one of those horrible cigars. Kristi, you come with me. There are some people I'd like you to meet. And I'll tell you about the time Nate nearly blew up the basement. He decided he wanted to be an inventor."

"I was nine," Nate said as his sister dragged him away.

"Well done, brother," Kristi heard her say.

She tucked her clutch firmly under her arm, tightened her grip on the stem of her wineglass and let Nate's mother lead her into the fray. This was going much better than she ever could have expected, and she realized she could easily get used to this. *Don't,* she reminded herself. A lot of real relationships didn't last. Fake ones didn't stand a chance.

THREE HOURS LATER, Kristi was in the kitchen, washing stemware by hand. The 1940s charm of the McTavish home had been maintained everywhere but the kitchen, which was a model of modern efficiency and a joy to work in.

Helen cleared counters, stowed leftover hors d'oeuvres and unopened bottles of sparkling water in the refrigerator and loaded the dishwasher while Nate and his father went through the house, gathering glasses, plates and crumpled napkins.

The evening had flown by, and in a way Kristi wished the party wasn't over. Helen had introduced her to numerous people as "my son's girlfriend, the owner of Ready Set Sold." She had handed out a surprising number of business cards—even Claire would have been impressed—and she had made contact with a woman who did upholstery and draperies. Kristi would be calling her on Monday to get more information about her rates and availability. The evening had been overwhelming and invigorating. She had not expected Nate's family to welcome her into their home and their lives with such genuine warmth, and she felt guilty as hell.

At one point during the evening, Nate's mother had shown her through the house, including a tour of the back garden. Everything Nate had told her about his mother's green thumb was true. The back garden was a private oasis, filled with flowering shrubs and fruit trees, bird feeders and an old cast-iron birdbath. In the back corner a tire swing hung from the branch of a big old chestnut tree. Nate's father had put it there when Nate and his sister were kids, and Molly and Martha loved to play on it now.

On Sunday she would get to see that firsthand because she and Nate were bringing the twins and Jenna here for Britt's birthday brunch.

"I think this is it," Nate said, setting an overloaded tray on the counter next to the sink.

"Where's your father?" Helen asked.

"He's having a nightcap out on the terrace."

"No cigars, I hope."

"No cigars," Nate said.

"Why don't you go join him?" Helen dumped soap in the dishwasher, closed the door and turned it on. "Kristi and I can finish up in here."

"No nightcaps for me. I have to drive home."

Kristi felt his hand slide beneath her hair, the light stroke of his thumb across the nape of her neck. *This is for his mother's benefit,* she reminded herself. *Not yours.* But that didn't lessen the sensations that shimmered along her spine.

"I think we're ready to call it a night," he said.

More shivers.

"Nate told me that your daughter is looking after Molly and Martha."

Kristi eased away from his touch and dried her hands on a kitchen towel. "She is. And we should really get home… back to Nate's, I mean…and see how they're doing."

Helen smiled. "Thank you for your help in here. I'll see you both on Sunday. It'll be good to see the girls, and I'm looking forward to meeting your daughter, too."

Kristi hadn't mentioned the brunch to Jenna yet. She had told her daughter that she and Nate were just friends, and that this evening was strictly casual. She wasn't sure she believed it herself, and she knew for sure Jenna wouldn't believe they were just friends if Nate was as attentive on Sunday as he had been tonight. So much for not being complicated.

Chapter Six

The evening had gone well, Nate thought as he took the on-ramp to the I-5, geared down and merged into the north-bound lane. Kristi had been quiet since they'd left his parents' place, though, and he wondered what she was thinking. Her silence made him a little uneasy, although he couldn't exactly say why.

Best way to find out what she's thinking is probably to ask. Even though he might not like the answer. "I hope you had an okay time tonight."

"I had fun," she said. "Your family's great. Your mother introduced me to lots of people, and I even made some business contacts."

Okay. She'd enjoyed herself, hit it off with his mother. All good. So why did he detect a "but"?

"But I'm not sure this was such a good idea."

And there it was. "Really? Why is that?"

He'd had reservations about tonight, but being with her had felt natural. So natural, he'd found himself wishing this was real. And since his mother and sister seemed genuinely taken with her, he was confident they would stop trying to fix him up with every single woman they encountered. "You really had that bad a time?"

"Oh, no. I enjoyed myself. It's been ages since I've gone out for something that wasn't related to my job or my daughter's school. I'm just worried that we've given your family the wrong idea."

"I hope we did." That had been the whole point.

"Your mother invited me to have lunch with her next week. Did she tell you?"

"No, she didn't." And he had not anticipated anything like that. "What did you say?"

"That I have a busy week lined up and I would have to check my calendar."

He relaxed a little. "Okay. So you'll tell her you're busy. That shouldn't be a problem."

"Will your mother settle for that and not keep asking?"

If his mother truly wanted to have lunch with Kristi, there wasn't an ice cube's hope in hell that she would let this drop. "We'll figure something out," he said. "Maybe I'll talk to her."

"Then you'd better talk to your sister, too, because she invited me to go shopping with her. She wants to redecorate the master suite in her condo, and now that you and I are together…her words, not mine…she's going to take advantage of having a 'decorator in the family.'" To drive the point home, Kristi added air quotes to the end of her sentence.

Well, hell. What could be a sticky situation with his mother just got more complicated. Helen McTavish might be deterred, hell's snowball aside, but Britt? Not a chance. She never took no for an answer.

"Britt can be persuasive but she had no right to ask you for free advice. I hope you didn't agree."

"She did say that if I ever need legal counsel—"

"Seriously?" He and Britt would definitely be having words over this. "Did she tell you she's a criminal defence lawyer?"

Kristi laughed at that. "Yes, but she said her firm handles other things—contracts, wills, real estate—and she'd be happy to set me up with another lawyer."

He gripped the steering wheel and stared at the tail-lights ahead of him. He had not seen any of this coming, although knowing his family as he did, he should have anticipated it. Now the solution to one problem had snow-balled into a bigger one.

"Did I mention that Jenna has also been invited for brunch on Sunday?"

"No. My mother didn't say anything. What did you tell her?"

"I couldn't think of an excuse why she couldn't be there so I said I'd bring her. I'm afraid the invitation caught me off guard."

He signaled for the next exit. "Do you think Jenna will mind?"

"I don't think so. I'm worried about giving her the wrong impression, though. She already thinks tonight was a date, and your family is convinced this is the real thing."

He appreciated why she didn't want to deceive her daughter. Molly and Martha were too young to understand the concept of dating, but Jenna knew the score. Kristi couldn't very well tell her this was an elaborate ruse to make their families stop setting them up with blind dates.

"If you would rather not go on Sunday, just say the word. I can tell my mother that you had a family thing come up and you couldn't get out of it." His mother and Britt would be disappointed. So would he.

Being with Kristi tonight had been a lot more enjoy-able than he'd expected, and convincing everyone that they were really dating had been a lot easier. Putting his arm around her, touching her hair from time to time—it all felt perfectly natural.

"I don't think lying to them is a good idea," she said. "No more than we already are."

"You're sure?"

"I am. And since I didn't think to get anything for your sister, I'll tell her the shopping trip is her birthday present."

"Thanks. I owe you."

She laughed. "You might regret that. You haven't met my family yet."

He glanced sideways and caught her smile, but he couldn't tell if she was joking or not.

"Do you mind if I ask you something?" Kristi said.

"Ask away."

"You told me your wife died. She must have been pretty young. What happened?"

To his surprise, he didn't mind talking about it. He did want some context, though. "Let me guess. My sister said it's been two years and about time I finally dived back into the dating pool. And my mother said that after two years, it would be good for Molly and Martha to have a female role model in their lives."

"You took the words right out of their mouths," Kristi said.

"Heather was diabetic, had been since childhood, and she'd had a kidney removed before we met. Her doctor warned that a pregnancy would be hard on her health. We should have been more careful. I mean, we *were* careful, but nothing's ever one hundred percent."

"Tell me about it. The last thing I expected to be at eighteen was a mother. We thought we were being careful—at least *I* thought we were being careful."

He gave her a quick side glance, recalling her earlier reference to Jenna's father's car. "Do you have any regrets?"

"Not now. There was a time when I wished my daughter didn't have a deadbeat for a dad. I know there are times she feels as though she's missing out, like when her friends' fathers are driving the car pool or running kids to the mall, but most of the time she's fine with not having him around."

Deadbeat. He'd heard her use that term once before, to describe him. Let it slide, he decided.

"But you were telling me about your wife," Kristi reminded him.

"Right. The pregnancy was a lot harder on her than anyone expected. By the time we found out we were having twins, it was too late…not that she would have done anything anyway. She really wanted children and thought it would be better to have them while she was young and still reasonably healthy.

"When it became obvious just how big a toll the pregnancy was taking, she was put on bed rest, and then the girls were delivered eight weeks early."

"Oh, Nate. That must have been hard."

"The girls were pretty tiny so they spent a couple of months in the neonatal unit. They were healthy and they were being well cared for, so we focused on getting Heather better. Only that didn't happen."

Kristi didn't respond, so he kept talking as he negotiated the familiar streets of his neighborhood.

"She only had the one kidney and it was failing. She started dialysis, and the doctors put her on a wait list for a transplant."

"That's awful. So many people don't understand how important it is to be an organ donor."

"Everyone in my family learned that pretty quickly. We all volunteered to be tested, but her mother was the only match. The girls were just a year old when Heather had the surgery. Everything looked good for the first few months, then her body rejected the new kidney. The doctors did everything they could but they couldn't save her."

He pulled into the driveway and turned off the engine.

Kristi put a hand on his arm. "Thank you for telling me. I had no idea. Your poor daughters…"

He covered her hand with his, not wanting to lose the connection. For the first time since those dark days, he thought about opening up, telling Kristi how devastated Heather's mother had been, how she considered her loss to be paramount to everyone else's, and that she now seemed to believe her sacrifice granted her some degree of ownership of his family. Could he say those things to Kristi? Should he? Or was he simply reacting to a pleasant evening in the company of a beautiful woman?

"Most of the time Heather was too sick to be with Molly and Martha, and they were too young to remember her." He stopped himself from saying more. Spilling his guts was not the way to keep this thing with Kristi casual and uncomplicated.

"I guess that would make it easier," she said. "But it's also sad they never knew their mother, that they never had a chance to make memories with her."

He'd never thought of it that way, and honestly, he didn't want to dwell on it now. And aside from a desire to change the subject, there was something he wanted to know, too. "Now do you mind if I ask you a question?"

"Not at all."

"I heard you talking on the phone the other day. I wasn't trying to eavesdrop, but you were in my office, and when I went to tell you we were on for tonight, you were telling someone you'd agreed to this date because there are no strings attached, and that you weren't taking a chance on another deadbeat."

She covered her face with her hands. "You heard that? Oh, Nate. I'm so sorry."

"So you do think I'm a—"

"No!" She dropped her hands and met his gaze head-on. "I wasn't talking about you. I was talking about men in general. My dad was a deadbeat, and then I did the same thing my mother did and married one. I have this lousy track record and I want something else for my daughter."

He felt bad for putting her on the spot. She was obviously embarrassed, but he was glad he asked. "Good to know," he said. "That I'm not a deadbeat, I mean. Not that the other men in your life are. Were." *You can stop talking anytime now.*

She touched his hand again and he liked it even better the second time around. "I'm so sorry you thought I was talking about you. No one could think that. You're raising two little kids on your own…you have an amazing career."

"And I'm a terrible housekeeper, I second-guess every parenting decision I make and I can't get my four-year-old to stop sucking her thumb." He'd never said those things out loud to anyone, and he hoped they didn't sound as pathetic to her as they did to him

"Kids don't come with a how-to manual. We have to follow our instincts and not be afraid to ask for help or advice when we need it. Jenna used to suck her thumb, too. I asked our pediatrician about it, and he told me it was perfectly normal and that kids grow out of it. And you know what? He was right. I can't remember when she stopped, but it feels like forever ago."

"Thanks. I needed to hear that." Would Alice back off if he mentioned the pediatrician?

Everything he'd ever attempted had come easily. Academia was second nature. He'd sailed through graduate school with high marks and scholarships. He got the first

faculty position he applied for. He'd never failed at anything except marriage and parenthood. Talking to Kristi
about it made him feel as though he was doing an okay
job after all.

He was glad she had asked about Heather, and he was
damn glad he'd asked about what she'd said on the phone.
Now he was done talking. He and Kristi were sitting angled in their seats, facing one another, her hand still on his.
He touched her arm, her skin soft and smooth beneath his
fingers. It wasn't enough. He followed the warmth till his
hand found the curve of her neck beneath the soft weight
of her hair, and when he leaned closer, she did the same.
The move caused his hand to slide a little higher, his thumb
now resting on the smoothness of her cheek.

She didn't say anything, didn't need to because her
eyes told him everything he wanted to know. If he kissed
her right now, she would let him. Would it be a mistake to
end a fake date with a real kiss? Of course it would. Did
he care? Hell no.

The kiss, at first too tentative to be considered inti-
mate, quickly turned into an exploration, an intoxicating
mix of taste and touch. Her luscious scent rushed through
him, and then she wound her arms around his neck as
though they belonged there. A first kiss had a steep learning curve. He wanted this one to be perfect, and it was.
He wanted it not to end, but it did.

"Wow." The single word floated past her lips and
brushed over his.

"You took the word right out of my mouth."

The coach lanterns on the front of the garage cast
enough light that he could see her smile.

"No regrets, I hope."

She shook her head. "None."

"We should go in."

"We should." Neither of them moved. Instead she nestled her head against his shoulder, and he wished the narrow space separating them wasn't taken up by the e-brake and stick shift. He wanted to touch her in places he shouldn't, and he wanted her to do the same for him.

If he'd been capable of using his head, he might have helped her out of the car and put an end to this fake date. But he wasn't thinking, at least not with his head. He kissed her again, a longer, deeper kiss that shut down the rest of his brain cells.

"I don't suppose there's any chance you still have that condom in your purse."

She pulled away. "Seriously? A couple of kisses and you think, you think—?"

Shit. He wanted to smack his head on the steering wheel. "Sorry. I think it's safe to say I wasn't thinking."

"But you think that because I'm a single mom, and because I had a condom in my bag that I'm…what? Easy?"

"I did *not* think that." Not completely. They'd just met, he hadn't known anything about her and he had sort of wondered. "I figured you were seeing someone."

"Well, I'm not."

"I know that now. And I think we agree that I'm an idiot?" A complete idiot who hadn't been with a woman in a very long time.

"Agreed. And for the record, I had a perfectly good reason for having that condom in my bag. And no, I don't have it with me now."

"You don't owe me an explanation—"

"Well, you're getting one. I signed up for a parenting class on how to have 'the talk' with kids."

"The talk?"

"The facts of life, the birds and bees…sex, birth control, abstinence."

Ah, *that* talk.

"My daughter is fourteen—she's getting interested in boys." She sighed as she said it. "Even worse, boys are interested in her. Mostly I want to talk to her about *not* getting involved with boys, not *that* way. She's way too young. But I also want her to know how to be safe, how to protect herself. How not to make the same mistakes I made."

"They have classes for that?"

"They do. I'm afraid I'm not a very good student, though. Jenna and I still haven't had the talk, which is why I was still carrying the stupid condom around with me."

Apparently the serotonin was wearing off and his brain was starting to function again. He wanted to ask how the condom factored into *the talk* but didn't dare ask. And then he experienced a mild sense of panic at the thought of someday having to have *the talk* with Molly and Martha. Luckily he had ten years to figure out how to handle that.

"Don't they tell kids about stuff like this in school?" One could always hope.

"They teach the biology of how it all works, but it's up to parents to help their kids make the decisions that are best for them."

Okay, that made sense, although it didn't make him any more confident about someday having to have this conversation with his own daughters. Maybe it would be easier if he'd had sons instead. No, it wouldn't. Not if his father was any kind of example. There had been no father-son talk. His dad had left his and Britt's upbringing to their mother, who'd been a stay-at-home mom and a great one at that. There'd been plenty of talk about treating girls well, being polite, being a gentleman. Looking back, he was damn sure his mother's between-the-lines message had been to avoid all situations that called for condoms.

"So in this parenting class, they give you all the information you need to have this conversation with your teenager?"

"Yes. They gave us pamphlets to help us talk to our kids about preventing STDs, unplanned pregnancies. The only problem is…" She paused, looked down at her hands now folded primly in her lap. "I haven't figured out how to initiate the conversation, and I'm not looking forward to demonstrating how to use a condom."

Surprise didn't come close to describing his reaction. *"Demonstrate?"*

"With a banana."

Laughter was not an appropriate adult response, but he couldn't help himself. "I thought stuff like that only happened on TV."

"I wish." She was laughing, too. "Now you know why I had a condom in my bag. And that I'm not as great a mom as I'd like to be."

"Don't." He held a finger to her lips. "You're smart, beautiful, and I can tell that you're a wonderful mom. You know exactly what you need to do with your daughter, and I envy that." He pulled his hand away and gave her a light, lingering kiss.

"Speaking of parents and kids, we should go inside and see how ours are doing."

She was right. He'd rather be alone with her, wanted to kiss her again, but he'd already moved too fast.

"The house is still standing…there were no frantic phone calls. Everything must have gone well."

"They're fine," Kristi said, looking a little sheepish. "I called Jenna earlier, from the powder room."

And there it was, proof that she was a better parent than he was, or at least a more conscientious one. It hadn't even occurred to him to call. Fake dates aside, it was good that Kristi had come into his life. He had a lot to learn.

KRISTI CLOSED THE front door of the town house, flipped the dead bolt home and let Hercules out of his carrier.

"You're awfully quiet," Jenna said.

"I'm tired." It was true. Who knew a fake date followed by a very real good-night kiss could crowd her thoughts and sap her energy? "It's been a busy week and I'm not used to being out this late." She pulled off her shoes and set them on the hall bench with her handbag. She was ready to turn in.

"Lots of nights you're up way later than this, sewing or working on one of your designs." Jenna scooped the dog into her arms and carried him into the kitchen. "And we could have been home half an hour ago if you guys hadn't been making out in the driveway."

"Jenna! Where did you get an idea like that?"

"I heard Nate's car pull into the driveway…you can hear one of those Beetles coming a mile away…but it was twenty minutes before you came inside."

Damn. It hadn't occurred to either of them that Jenna might hear the car. So much for setting a good example. "We were talking."

She followed her daughter into the kitchen in time to catch her rolling her eyes.

"It wasn't a date and we weren't…" *Yes, it was. And yes, you were.*

"He seems nice." Jenna got a bottle of water out of the fridge and unscrewed the cap.

"He is nice. And we're invited to have Sunday brunch with his family," Kristi said, hoping to change the subject.

"Cool."

"You don't mind?"

"Not if you don't mind me tagging along on one of your dates." Jenna grinned as she took a sip of water.

There was no point persisting with an argument she couldn't win. "Do you have plans tomorrow?"

"Studying for one more final. Math." She wrinkled her nose. "And then Abbie and I want to go to the mall in the afternoon. Can you drop me off? Her mom said she'll bring me home?"

These days Jenna and her best friend were spending a lot of time with two boys named Matt and Jordan. According to the parenting class, there was safety in numbers. Did four hormonal teenagers constitute sufficient numbers to ensure safety?

"Will it just be you and Abbie?"

"Don't know. Probably."

"I need to work for a couple of hours tomorrow. I suggested that Nate buy a new sofa for his family room—"

"Good idea. The one he has now is pretty gross. The cushions are all squishy, and the material on one of the arms is nearly worn off."

"He said Gemmy chewed on it when she was a puppy. Which is why he's agreed to buy a new one. It'll really spruce up the family room, and he can take it to their new house."

Jenna absently stroked the top of Hercules's head. "It's weird that he'd want to sell it. Did you know there's a pool in the backyard? I would kill to live in a house like that."

That makes two of us, Kristi thought, although she would never let Jenna think she was anything but completely content with their town house. "Will you stay with the girls for a couple of hours in the morning? Sam will be there, too. She's going to start painting."

"I guess. What about the mall?"

It seemed like a fair exchange. "You help out in the morning and I'll drive you to the mall in the afternoon."

"It's a deal. Can I take my study notes to Nate's?"

"Can you study and keep an eye on the girls at the same time?"

"No problem. They're pretty cute kids and they keep each other entertained."

Molly and Martha had completely different personalities, but they were very close. That was probably normal for twins, but it might also have something to do with growing up without a mom. Kristi's chest tightened, as it had when Nate told her how his wife died. So sad.

"They are pretty adorable." Kristi stifled a yawn. "I think I'll turn in." She would take her laptop with her and go over her notes for tomorrow to make sure she had everything she needed.

"I'm going to see what's on TV."

"Don't be up too late. I'd like to get an early start in the morning."

Upstairs, she slipped out of the green dress that had been such a hit with Nate's mother and sister, and pulled on an old T-shirt and a pair of boxers. After she removed her makeup and brushed out her hair, she climbed into bed, turned on her computer and opened the file for Nate's house. She absently scrolled through her lists and photographs, but her thoughts were elsewhere.

The kiss had been an unexpected but welcome end to their this-is-not-a-date date, and if any other man had asked if she had a condom, she'd be heading for the hills by now. Instead he had opened the door to a conversation about parenting that they might not have had otherwise. She was glad he'd talked to her. He had everything going for him—intelligence, incredible good looks, confidence—and yet when it came to raising his kids, by his own admission, he second-guessed every decision. Even worse, she suspected he had some residual guilt over his wife's death. The mother-in-law who had donated a kidney and lost her daughter anyway might have something to do with that.

Kristi thought back to her brief marriage to Jenna's father. Derek hadn't taken responsibility for anything, not even the condom that, looking back, he had most likely been carrying around in his wallet for months. No wonder the stupid thing hadn't worked. Did he ever feel guilty for bringing Jenna into the world and then bailing on her and her mother? If he did, he sure never let on. They hadn't heard from him since he'd called the day after Christmas. He wasn't working—no surprise there—so he had no money for gifts, although judging by his slurred words and the raucous racket in the background, there was money for partying. Not wanting to listen to his usual string of flimsy excuses, she had handed the phone over to Jenna.

Their conversation had been short and, as was always the case, Jenna didn't want to talk about it afterward. Kristi prided herself on having a good relationship with her daughter. She worked hard to maintain it and it broke her heart that in this one area, perhaps the one that mattered most, Jenna refused to open up. Kristi had always been careful not to say anything negative about him, in spite of the fact that Derek really was a deadbeat.

The opposite of Nate in pretty well every way possible. Thankfully he'd called her on the deadbeat reference because she would hate for him to believe that's what she thought of him. When it came to measuring a man's character, Nate and Derek were at opposite ends of the yardstick.

She turned off her laptop, set it on the nightstand and snuggled in between the sheets. Until tonight, she would have told herself that Nate McTavish's parenting skills were none of her business. That kiss had changed everything.

No, not *everything*. She was a single mom, determined as ever to set an example for her teenage daughter. A single mom who didn't need a man in her life. But she could still help Nate see that he was doing a great job as a single dad. And if that involved another kiss, or two, so be it.

Chapter Seven

Sam's old utility truck was parked in front of Nate's house when Kristi and Jenna arrived the next morning.

"Cool," Jenna said as they pulled up behind it. "Do you think she brought her little boy with her?"

"No, he's at home with his father, or maybe the nanny. Won't you have your hands full with the twins?"

"I guess. He's about their age, though. I bet they'd get along great."

True. But Sam would be working, so the twins and the two dogs would be plenty of responsibility for Jenna, especially if she planned to study, too.

"Can you carry Hercules in with you? I'll get my bag out of the back."

Inside, Sam's toolboxes and the wallpaper steamer lined one side of the foyer. In the family room the TV was on, the tent flap was open and the sofa bed had been unfolded. Nate had said he would sleep there, closer to the girls. Gemmy was sprawled on the bed. Nate and the girls were nowhere to be seen, but Molly's and Martha's voices drifted in through the open patio door. They were in their playhouse, Kristi guessed, and Nate would be in his greenhouse.

Jenna set the pet carrier on the sofa bed and unzipped it. "Here we are, Herc. Come on out and see your girlfriend."

The huge dog sat up, making the springs sag. Hercules popped his head out and Gemmy's ears perked forward.

"It's kind of cute that they get along so well," Jenna said.

That was true. Last night Kristi and Nate had come home and been amused to find the dogs curled up together in Gemmy's bed, a snarl of tattered blankets in the corner of the family room.

"Would you go out and let Nate and the girls know we're here? I need to talk to Sam about today's work plan."

"Will do." Jenna dumped her math books on the bed next to Hercules's carrier, gave each dog a treat and headed outside.

Kristi found Sam in the girls' bedroom, kneeling on the floor, unscrewing the covers of the electrical outlets and dumping them in a small plastic bucket.

"Good morning. You're an early bird."

Sam checked her watch and grinned. "And you're not."

"Very funny. I said we'd be here by nine, and we almost made it."

"So, I met your professor. Seems like a nice guy."

Here we go. "He is." Best to ignore the reference to him being hers.

"How was your date last night?"

"It wasn't a date."

"Right." Sam stood up and shoved the screwdriver in her back pocket. "How was your fake date?"

Kristi closed the door behind her. She did not want anyone eavesdropping on this conversation. Not Nate, and especially not Jenna. "It was good—his family's great. He…"

"What?"

"He kissed me." She'd planned to keep that to herself, but it popped out like the cork from a shaken bottle of champagne.

"Ha! I knew it."

"You knew what?"

"That it was a real date." Sam picked up a putty knife and opened a pail of patching compound. "How was it?"

"The date?"

"The kiss, silly."

Magical. Heart-stopping. Best kiss ever. "It was nice."

Sam was grinning again. "Just 'nice'? That's too bad. I'd have guessed that a man who looks like he does could soften up a girl's bones without any effort at all."

"Okay, it was nicer than nice. By a factor of ten, at least. But it was unexpected. I mean, we agreed this was strictly a matter of convenience, no strings attached."

"Sounds simple, but we both know chemistry doesn't work that way. The attraction between two people doesn't have a whole lot to do with logic. Actually, it kind of defies it."

True. Sam herself was living proof of that. Last winter she had reconnected with AJ Harris, a man from her past, the man who had fathered her son, Will. They were now married and happily ensconced, with Sam's mother and Will's nanny, in the house that Ready Set Sold had been hired to renovate when AJ considered selling it.

Kristi was thrilled for Sam. She'd had a hard life, and if anyone deserved to have her happily-ever-after, she did. It's what every woman wanted and it's what Kristi promised herself she could have, *after* she finished raising her daughter.

"Have you talked to Claire this morning?" Kristi asked.

"No, have you?"

"No. She's been super busy with new clients looking for properties. She hasn't seen this place yet. After she saw the photographs, she decided to hold off on an appraisal until we have most of the work done."

"Good idea. Along with being the busiest woman on the planet, she's also been getting a lot of grief from her ex. She said he keeps calling and bugging her about stuff."

"That guy is such a jerk. I hope he's not trying to get back together with her."

"No, thank God. He wants her to sell their condo."

"He probably needs the money."

"And Claire doesn't. She says she isn't ready to sell it, and when she is, it'll be on her terms."

"He should have taken all of that into account before he hooked up with his new girlfriend." The guy was a two-timing weasel and Kristi had absolutely no sympathy for him.

"She'll work it out. I've been hoping she'll meet someone and put this behind her."

"She might if she wasn't so busy."

Sam pulled out a couple of picture hangers with the claw end of her hammer and troweled some plaster over the holes. "We're all busy. I used to think that working and taking care of my mom was all I could manage. Now I have a home, a husband and a son, and yes, I'm busy. Never been busier, actually, but I've never been happier, either. Claire deserves to have that."

Kristi couldn't agree more. "We all do."

"Now that you're dating Nate, maybe you will."

And we're back to that. "Clever, but I don't see it happening."

"What about the kiss?"

"It was just a kiss."

"It was so *not* just a kiss. You said so yourself. Maybe you should give this thing a chance. Give him a chance."

Now that Sam was happily ensconced in a beautiful home with the love of her life, she wanted the same for everyone else. Sure, Kristi wanted what Sam had, someday, but for now she was happy with her life as it was.

"The kiss just happened, caught us off guard. We're both on the same page about this being a way to make our families stop matchmaking."

Sam was paying close attention to patching the walls but she wasn't hiding her amusement. "And if you say it out loud often enough, it's bound to be true."

They could go around and around this issue all day, and Sam would still think this thing with Kristi and Nate was something it wasn't. "I should see if Nate's ready to leave. Jenna's watching the girls, and both dogs are here, too."

"No problem. Tell her to give me a shout if she needs a hand with anything. And have fun."

"There'll be no fun. This is strictly business."

Sam opened the door and gave her a playful shove into the hallway. "Get going, and whatever you do, don't have any fun."

NATE COULDN'T REMEMBER the last time he'd been in a furniture store. He completely agreed that a new sofa would spruce up the current family room as well as the next home he and the girls moved to, and almost anything would be an improvement over the one he had now. It was a hand-me-down from Heather's parents, hauled out of their basement and into the family room after he and Heather got married and bought the house. Like everything else, the plan had been to buy a new one after they were settled and the babies were born, but like all the other plans, it had been put on hold temporarily, and then permanently. Until now.

This morning he was grateful to have Kristi with him because gazing across what appeared to be an acre of furniture was overwhelming. She wanted to bring him here

because it was her favorite place for good-quality affordable furniture designed for everyday living. She breezed
through the store with confidence and style, and he was
content to trail behind, taking in her scent and admiring
those dynamite legs. She was wearing lower heels than that
first day she'd come to the house, but he still liked the way
they emphasized the smooth curves and slender ankles.

She stopped unexpectedly and swung around to check
the price tag attached to the arm of a brown sectional, and
he almost ran into her. Instinctively he reached out, put
his hand on her waist. She smiled up at him, green eyes
sparkling, lips within easy kissing distance.

"What do you think?" she asked. She was talking about
the sofa.

He was thinking about something else. "It looks good."

She took a seat and patted the cushion next to her. "Give
it a try."

He sat, bounced a couple of times. "Comfy. I'll take it."

"You can't buy the first sofa you see."

"Why not?"

"Because there might be something better." She ran a
hand over the sofa. "Nice fabric, though. It'll stand up to
a lot of wear and tear."

"I like brown. It won't show the dirt, or the dog hair."

That made her laugh.

"You have no idea how much I hate housework. It's a
lot to juggle…the girls, my job, the house."

"I know what you mean."

Of course she did. She was single-handedly raising a
teenager who he suspected, having met Jenna, could be
a real handful.

"This will probably sound sexist," he said. "But women
are always better at this."

"Not always. Hardly ever, actually. You're doing a—"

"You look like a happy couple." A salesman in a gray suit stood in front of them. "Anything I can do to help?"

Damn the interruption. He and Kristi were in the store to buy furniture, but he liked hearing her say he didn't stink at being a single dad as badly as everyone else seemed to think he did. If she said it a few more times, he might even start to believe her.

He stood, held out a hand to help Kristi, amused to see that the "happy couple" remark had her blushing.

"We're here to buy a new couch for the family room," Nate said. It was too complicated to explain that they weren't a couple. "This is the first one we've looked at."

"My name's Walt." The guy pulled a card from his pocket and handed it to Nate. "Let me know if you have any questions."

"Thanks," Kristi said. "We'd like to keep browsing."

"Sure thing. I'll just let you know that this particular model happens to be on sale, and it's available in several colors." Walt handed her a set of fabric swatches. "You folks take a look around and let me know if I can be of any assistance."

Nate wondered if this one was a sofa bed. Not that he needed a pullout in the family room, but sitting on it with Kristi had him thinking about beds.

"We'll do that." With a hand on Kristi's back, he guided her away, hoping Walt wouldn't follow them.

Twenty minutes and half a dozen couches later, they were back at the brown sectional.

"So you still think this is the one?" Kristi asked.

Walt, who had been hovering the whole time, closed in. "Looks like you folks have made a decision."

"I think we have."

"Well then, why don't you follow me over to the sales desk and we'll get this taken care of."

They crossed the showroom floor behind Walt. To Nate's surprise, this furniture shopping expedition had been painless, with the exception of Walt's dismal attempt to schmooze. It helped that Kristi seemed to understand Nate's taste better than he did.

The sectional he'd settled on was everything she'd said it would be, affordable and versatile. Walt keyed the sale into his computer, assured them there was one in the warehouse and promised it would be delivered on Tuesday.

"Why don't we take a look at children's bedroom furniture while we're here?" Kristi asked after they parted company with Walt. "I'm not suggesting you need to buy any, but I like the way their displays are set up. They're like actual bedrooms and might give us some ideas."

"Sure." Since she didn't expect him to make any more decisions or purchases, he was happy to agree. Plus it extended their time together...and what could he say? He enjoyed spending time with her.

What she'd said about the children's furniture displays was bang on. He could easily see any of them working for Molly and Martha if it weren't for all their clothes and toys.

"Have you decided what to do with all of those stuffed animals?" she asked.

He had not. "I wish their grandparents would stop giving them to us, but I hate to ask the girls to get rid of the ones they already have."

Kristi pulled her camera out of her bag. "Let me show you something."

She turned it on, scrolled through some photos, then handed it to him. On the monitor was a picture of Martha sitting on her bed, smiling happily, surrounded by her stuffies. Kristi clicked to the next photograph, a similar one of Molly.

"Because we were moving everything out of their room,

I asked each of them to pick their three favorites. Molly quickly chose three. Martha really only had one—"

"The purple dinosaur," Nate said.

"Barney." Kristi grinned. "She finally chose two more, and then we bagged up the rest and hauled them into the spare room. I took the photographs because I thought that if you and the girls agreed to donate those stuffed animals to charity, I would have these photographs framed for them. That way they would have a permanent reminder of them but without the clutter."

He liked that idea. A lot. What he didn't like was the guilt that threatened as he wondered what Alice would think.

Kristi must have read his mind. "I know you're worried about what your mother-in-law might say, but the toys belong to the girls now and the ultimate decision about what to do with them is really yours, and theirs."

Taking a stand sounded so sensible, so easy when she said it, but she didn't know the half of it. Dealing with the toys would be much simpler than the beauty pageant. In fact, maybe the toys would be a good practice run.

"The photographs are a great idea, but I don't know if the girls will agree to get rid of all the toys."

Kristi's smile suggested she knew better. "Why don't we try this? After the room is painted and we move the girls back in, we'll leave the stuffies in the bags in the spare room. All the too-small clothing and dress-up clothes will be pared down, and I guarantee they'll love the room without the clutter because they'll have space to play, and when they look for something they'll be able to find it."

Everything she said made sense, but would she be there when he told Alice to stop buying toys and Britt to stop bringing dress-up clothes?

She seemed to read his mind.

"If it helps, I'll back you up when you tell them." Her grin had a mischievous little twist to it. "Since everyone already believe we're dating, I don't think that's too much of a stretch."

He wanted to kiss her, right there in the middle of the furniture store. "It's a deal," he said instead. He felt a little as though he was taking the coward's way out, but when it came to his mother-in-law, that worked for him.

"What do you think of these storage solutions?" Kristi asked.

The display room had a closet outfitted with cubbies, bars for hanging clothes and upper shelves filled with large baskets. It looked perfect, and pretty much the opposite of what the girls had now.

"I like it. How much will something like this cost?"

"The components are sold separately, and they can really add up. I've already discussed this with Sam, and she can build something very similar for a fraction of the price. I'll pick up some dollar-store baskets to go in the cubbies, and the girls can use those for everyday things. The larger baskets overhead can store out-of-season clothes."

The house would be so well organized, he might not want to sell. "We won't want to leave them behind."

"You won't have to. Sam will build everything in sections so they're easy to move and can be adapted to any closet."

"I've never met a female handyman...person...handy-woman."

"She's an amazing carpenter, but I don't think there's anything she can't do. Painting, installing light fixtures, fixing leaking taps—Sam does it all, and with so much attention to detail. Our clients are always really happy with her work."

The same could be said for Kristi. He should probably tell her that, and he wasn't sure why he didn't. "Good to know" was all he could manage.

"Claire is pretty incredible, too, and super busy. She's going to swing by sometime next week to take a look at your place. You'll meet her then."

Claire was the real estate agent, the one who was going to appraise the house and get it on the market, and then there'd be no turning back. For the first time in what felt like forever, the weight he'd been shouldering was starting to lighten. Maybe he really could make a comfortable home for himself and the girls. With Kristi's help, that is. He hadn't quite figured out how to do this on his own, but maybe someday.

KRISTI WAS GLAD to see Sam's truck was still parked in front of the house when they returned from shopping. After they'd left the furniture store Nate had insisted on taking her out for lunch, and although she should have said no, she'd said yes. She'd called Jenna to make sure she had everything under control, and Sam to let her know she'd be back a little later than expected.

They'd gone to a casual deli-style cafeteria close to the university and not far from his place. They ate made-to-order sandwiches while they talked about her plans for the house…so it had really been a working lunch. Then they'd shared a brownie with whipped cream for dessert. One brownie and two forks felt more like a date, but wasn't.

Nate was easy to talk to, and more relaxed than he'd been since she'd started working for him. Sitting in the café with her, he wasn't a man struggling to keep house, decipher the needs of two little girls, meet his family's demands. He didn't even have to be a university professor, although she suspected that's the role he was most com-

fortable in. And by the time lunch was over, she was more
intrigued by Nate McTavish than ever, and far more than
common sense dictated.

Now, back at his place, she reminded herself that she
had a job to do.

"What are your plans for the afternoon?" Nate asked.

She ran through her mental checklist. "We should
empty your office so Sam can strip the wallpaper. Will
you have time to help with that?"

"Already done. I finished it last night."

"Wow. I'm impressed. I'd like to tackle the foyer closet
this afternoon, and Sam and I will do a walk-through before she leaves so she can make a list of the other things
that need to be done."

"Let me know what I can do to help."

"Oh, believe me. We will."

They sat a moment longer without saying anything,
listening to the Saturday sounds of the neighborhood. A
lawn mower, someone hammering, boys shooting hoops
in a driveway down the block. Last night they'd sat like
this in the dark and he had kissed her. Today they were out
in the open for all the neighbors to see. Neither of them
was ready for that kind of PDA, as Jenna liked to call it.

"We should go in," she said. This time she didn't wait
for him to come around and open her door.

The house was quiet when they went inside. Almost
too quiet. The family room-turned-campground was still
a chaotic mess of camping gear.

Nate looked inside the tent and laughed. "Take a peek."

Gemmy, sprawled on her side on top of Molly's and
Martha's sleeping bags, filled the entire space. Hercules
was curled up under her chin. Both were sound asleep.
Kristi pulled out her camera and snapped a photograph of
them. "This has to be the cutest thing ever."

The patio doors were open and voices drifted in from the backyard.

"The kids must be out in the playhouse," Nate said. "I'll go check on them."

"I'll come with you and let Jenna know I'm back. She needs a ride to the mall to meet her friend."

They walked together across the patio and found the three girls crowded into the playhouse. The twins each wore a dress that flowed to the floor. Molly's was bright shimmery turquoise and Martha's was a lavender sequined number. A sash fashioned from a scarf was draped diagonally across the top of each girl's dress.

Jenna had combed out their pigtails and given each girl a unique hairdo. The contents of her makeup bag were strewn across the top of a little table. Molly's vivid aqua eye shadow and bright pink blush coordinated with her dress, and Martha's purple-rimmed eyes matched hers.

"Daddy!" Molly twirled and curtsied. "Look at us! Jenna did our makeup."

Kristi had to press her lips together to keep from laughing out loud. They looked a little outlandish and absolutely adorable. "You guys look so sweet. Jenna did a great job of—"

One glance at Nate wiped the smile off Kristi's face. He was not impressed. He was angry. Really angry.

"Molly. Martha. Get out of those clothes and in the house, now."

"Daddy, we're playing," Martha said. "Me an' Molly are beauty queens."

"In the house," he repeated. "I want you to go in the bathroom and scrub that makeup off your faces. Now."

Molly struck a defiant pose. "I don't want to."

"Now." He backed away from the playhouse door and waited, indicating he wasn't taking no for an answer.

Jenna hastily swept her makeup into the case and zipped it up. "Go on, girls. You need to do what your dad says."

Martha wriggled out of her dress.

"Why do we got to go in?" Molly asked.

"Because I said so."

Because? Kristi cringed.

Molly wasn't giving up that easily. "We're still playing."

What to do? Kristi wondered. Step in or stay out of it? If she sided with the girls, Nate would think she was interfering. If she sided with him, Jenna would think she'd done something wrong. That made staying out of the argument the best plan. The kids were just having some harmless fun and she didn't understand why Nate was making it such a big deal, but she'd be wise to let things slide and try talking to him about it when they were alone.

"You can find another game to play *after* you're cleaned up."

Jenna rolled her eyes.

Kristi gave her daughter a reassuring smile and a warning look that said, *Let this one go.* The last thing they needed was for Jenna to tell Nate that this was a load of crap.

Molly stomped barefoot out of the playhouse. "I want to play dress-up with Jenna. She's cool."

Kristi didn't know what Nate thought of her daughter, but she'd bet *cool* wasn't on the list.

Jenna gathered up her things and followed Molly, bending down to fit through the door. Kristi put a reassuring arm around her shoulder. "Let me handle this," she whispered.

Nate held out his hands to his daughters. Martha took one, but Molly pulled away and grabbed Kristi's instead. They trooped inside, a sullen-faced Jenna bringing up the rear. Nate hustled both girls, Molly still protesting loudly, down the hallway to the main bathroom.

"I'll go wait in the van." Jenna grabbed her math books off the counter and stormed out the front door, leaving Kristi standing alone in the middle of the family room with only the sound of Gemmy snoring inside the tent.

What the hell had just happened? She couldn't even guess, but there'd be no point trying to talk to Nate until he'd calmed down. For now she didn't want to keep Jenna waiting, but she had to let Sam know she was back, and that she was leaving again to run Jenna to the mall.

She tapped lightly on the twins' bedroom door and let herself in.

"You're back," Sam said, pulling her earphones out of her ears. "What's up?"

Kristi closed the door behind her and filled Sam in on the dress-up fiasco. "Nate has them in the bathroom now, scrubbing off their makeup."

"Huh. That's kind of over-the-top, but he must have his reasons."

"I'm sure he does, but he didn't have to freak out. Poor Jenna's sulking out in the van. I'll have to smooth things over because we're having brunch with Nate's family tomorrow."

"I'm sure it'll be fine," Sam said. "How was lunch?"

"Good. Really nice, actually. And then we got here and everything went south." Kristi looked around the room. "You're putting on primer already? At this rate we'll easily get the job wrapped up in a week or so, maybe less."

"That's the beauty of fast-drying patching compound." Sam set her paint roller on the edge of the tray and perched on the end of a sawhorse. "You might be finished with the house in a week, but I have a feeling you and Nate will be seeing each other after that."

Half an hour ago as they'd bumped forks over a brownie, Kristi would have agreed. He was the sexiest, smartest man she'd ever met. He was grounded, interested in all sorts of things, and contrary to her idea of a stereotypical professor, he had a great sense of humor. About some things, anyway.

"I wouldn't count on it. He's really angry, and so is Jenna."

Sam popped the lid off a Tupperware container and took out a carrot stick. "Want one?" she asked.

"No, thanks."

Sam crunched the carrot. "I can see you're into this guy—this wouldn't bother you if you weren't—but don't make it into a big deal, because it isn't."

"I just met him," Kristi reminded her. "What if this is how he reacts all the time? I can't handle that."

"And you shouldn't. All you need to do right now is relax and get to know him. If he turns out to be a jerk... or a deadbeat," Sam said with a wink, "then don't see him anymore."

Sam was right. Kristi had never let herself get crazy over a man, not since her divorce. What was different this time? She wasn't ready to examine that question too closely. "When did you get so smart?" she asked instead.

"When I let the man I love tear down my fortress. I thought I was protecting myself, but I was really just hiding, making excuses for not living my life. He saved me. I'm guessing you and Nate can do that for each other. If you'll let him, that is."

Kristi hugged her. "I'm so happy for you. It's a real-life fairy tale, and if anyone deserves a happy ending, it's you."

"So do you, hon. You and Jenna. Don't be too quick to slam the door this time."

Kristi's BlackBerry buzzed. It was a text message from her daughter. Can we go now?

"That's Jenna."

"I'll hold down the fortress till you get back," Sam said, giving her a sly wink. "Just don't slam that door on your way out."

"Subtle as always. I'll be back in an hour."

Chapter Eight

The mall parking lot was busier than usual for a Saturday afternoon. People must be getting ready for summer vacation, Kristi thought as she scanned the row ahead for a parking spot.

Jenna's cell phone buzzed. "It's a text from Abbie. She's meeting me at the main entrance. You can drop me off there."

"Is she already here?" Kristi asked. "If not, I'll wait with you till she arrives."

"Mom! You're treating me like a baby. I can be on my own for two minutes."

"What if something happens and she doesn't show up? I don't want you hanging around the mall on your own, and I don't want to have to come back for you. Sam and I have a lot to do this afternoon."

"How much longer do you have to work there?"

"Another week or so. Why?"

"'Cause he's a jerk. No way am I babysitting for him again."

Kristi let the remark about Nate slide. "He pays you, and I thought you liked the girls."

"Yeah, they're cute. But Nate totally flipped out about me putting makeup on them. What's that all about? It's not like I got them tattoos or had their ears pierced."

He had overreacted, no question about that. "I'm sure this is just a misunderstanding," Kristi said, even though she didn't really believe it. "I'll talk to him when I get back, smooth things over."

"Whatever." Jenna's phone buzzed again. "It's Abbie. There she is, right over there."

Kristi pulled into a loading zone and waved to her daughter's friend. "Her mom's picking you up, right?"

Jenna was already out of the van. "Yup."

"What time?"

"Four-thirty." The door slammed.

"I'll be home by five," Kristi yelled.

Jenna's wave didn't indicate whether or not she'd heard.

Kristi scanned the shoppers streaming past Abbie. There was no sign of the two boys they'd been hanging out with, but that didn't mean they weren't waiting inside or planning to show up later.

"She's a good kid," Kristi said out loud. She did a quick shoulder check before pulling away. She could trust Jenna to make good decisions, but they still needed to have that talk. "And you need to do it soon."

She would talk to Nate, too. She couldn't understand his being annoyed about the makeup. After all, he was fine with the dress-up clothes. Something about the makeup had set him off, and she wanted to find out why. Partly because she wanted to get to know him better, especially if they were going to keep up this charade of dating but not dating, but mostly because of the way he'd treated Jenna. She was just a kid, after all. She'd meant no harm, and caused none as far as Kristi was concerned. Nate owed Jenna an apology, and Kristi didn't mind telling him.

"THAT'S BETTER," NATE said to the girls after their faces were clean and their hair brushed and put back into little-girl pigtails. As usual, Molly's were a little lopsided because she wouldn't sit still.

Martha was still pouting. "We were playing. We weren't being bad."

"I know, sweetie. But I don't want you wearing makeup."

"Why?" Molly asked. "Grandma Alice put makeup on us and you didn't get mad."

Oh, yes, he had. And now it was also clear that Alice had filled their heads with this pageant nonsense, otherwise they wouldn't be dressing up as "beauty queens." He should have called her the day she'd dropped off the head shots and told her no. Instead he'd used the house renovation as an excuse to put off the confrontation, and now he'd made an ass of himself in front of Kristi and Jenna.

"Why can't we wear makeup?" Molly asked again.

"Because you're too young."

"It's just pretend," Martha said. Was it his imagination, or had she become more talkative, even a little more assertive since Kristi had come into their lives? Right away he'd noticed that Kristi wouldn't let Molly do her sister's talking for her. Something he should have insisted on long ago, even though it meant having two headstrong little girls questioning his decisions.

"I know you were just playing, but you don't need makeup for that. You can use your imaginations."

"We had makeup at Halloween."

"That's different."

"Why?"

"Because it just is." He took both girls by the hand and walked them down the hallway to the family room. "How would you like to watch a movie? We still have the DVD about rain-forest animals we borrowed from the library."

"Are you going to watch with us?" Martha asked.

He supposed he could, at least until Kristi got back. Then he'd need to take her aside and apologize. He flipped open the plastic case and slid the disc into the player. "I'll get it started for you. Then if Sam doesn't need me to help with anything, I'll come back and watch."

"Sam has a lot of tools," Martha said. "I'm going to be a carpenter when I grow up."

"You are?" Not if he had anything to say about it. His daughters were going to college, not trade school, and definitely not beauty school, but that conversation could wait. He recalled, with a certain degree of distaste, what Kristi'd said last night about needing to have "the sex talk" with her daughter. At least talking about education and careers would be a lot easier.

Molly bounced onto the sofa next to her sister. "I'm going to be like Jenna and wear makeup and be pretty and get a cell phone and a boyfriend."

Martha's pigtails bounced in agreement.

And we're back where we started, Nate thought. How did parents get their young daughters to understand that what was inside their heads had far more value than what was on the outside? Did they have classes for that?

He picked up the remote and pressed Play. "How do you know Jenna has a boyfriend?"

"'Cause he wrote something on her phone."

"And she said it was from her boyfriend?" he asked, hoping he sounded casual.

"Nope. She just said it was from a boy."

"His name's Matt."

"But pretty girls like Jenna get boyfriends." Seriously? When had Molly become an expert on teen dating?

"Look at Herc and Gemmy." Martha pointed at the dogs sleeping in the tent. "He's her boyfriend."

Nate had to smile at that. If there was ever an unlikely

pair, these two dogs were it. They'd really hit it off, but he still couldn't believe his four-year-olds were talking about boyfriends.

"The program's starting," he said. "Can you hear it okay or do you want me to turn it up?"

"Up." Molly reached for the remote. "I can do it."

Of course she could. He handed it to her. "I'll be down the hall if you need me."

The girls were already engrossed in the opening segment of a pair of orangutans picking nits from one another's fur. Too late now to worry about whether the film would demonstrate how primates made babies. He could already hear the questions. *Daddy, why...* And as usual, he wouldn't know how to answer.

SAM WAS IN the girls' room rolling primer on the walls, and it looked as though she was almost finished.

"Nice work," he said. She'd only started this morning and the room looked better already.

"I have a system," she said, without taking her eyes off the paint roller. "We like to get in and out with minimal disruption so our clients can sell their homes and get on with their lives."

Now that Kristi was "in," he was in no hurry to have her out, although after his earlier outburst, she'd likely want the opposite. He hated to think about how badly he'd behaved, and he had to apologize as soon as she came back.

"Is there anything you'd like me to do?"

"It'd be great if you could give me a hand moving the bookshelves out of your office." Sam stepped back from the wall and surveyed her work. Apparently satisfied, she wrapped her paint roller in a plastic bag and set it on the tarp-covered floor. "I'll clean this later."

She picked up a clipboard and checked an item off her

list. "Kristi asked me to talk to you about new shelving. Something with a lower profile instead of the floor-to-ceiling, wall-to-wall unit you have in here now."

"I've had this since I was a student. It was cheap and it served its purpose, but I won't miss it." Especially since, now that it was empty, it looked like something that belonged in a student's dorm room. "I'm not sure what I'll do with it but I'll put it in the garage for now."

"I can help you move it out there, and I'll bet Kristi can sell it for you."

"Really?" Someone would pay good money for this?

"She lists items on a couple of online sites. You'd be surprised what people will buy if it's priced right."

He didn't think there was anything Kristi could do that would surprise him. Without talking they dismantled the shelving unit and stacked the parts in the hallway, but he finally felt the need to break the silence. "How did you get into this kind of work?"

"From a woodworking elective I took in high school. There was just me and my mom in those days and she wasn't well enough to work, so there was no money for me to go to college. My teacher told me about an apprenticeship program, which meant I could learn on the job and have an income. I love what I do, so it was definitely the best option for me."

He had done his homework before he hired Ready Set Sold. The portfolio on their website confirmed that Sam was also extremely good at what she did. So was Kristi, and no doubt the third partner was every bit as accomplished.

"One of my girls just said she'd like to be a carpenter when she grows up." He wanted what was best for his girls and as far as he was concerned, that was college. But after what Sam said about her career choice, maybe he needed to revise his assumptions about what having "the best" meant. "Martha's impressed that you have so many tools."

Sam laughed. "Kids do love tools. My son is three and a half, a little younger than your girls, I think, and he can't get enough of them."

"What's his name?"

"William. We call him Will."

"It must be hard, doing the work you do plus running a business and raising a child at the same time."

"I don't think any parent has an easy job, but I'm one of the lucky ones. My husband's a writer, so he mostly works at home, and we have a live-in nanny who takes care of the whole family."

After Heather died he considered hiring a nanny or a housekeeper, and in the end he'd ruled it out because he hadn't wanted anyone else around. Relying on Alice and Fred to help with the girls when they were babies had been a mistake, but now that the girls were older he liked having them at the university's day care. And he was content to look after the house himself, even though he wasn't doing the greatest job. And then Kristi breezed in, and overnight all that had changed.

"It must be nice to have a creative outlet like this," he said.

"Kristi's the creative one in the business. She can walk into a home and immediately come up with a design that suits the client and still has broad appeal for prospective buyers. She tells me what she wants and I make it happen."

"She does have a good eye for detail." At the furniture store, he had liked everything she'd shown him. In fact she knew what would work for him and his family far better than he did.

"Kristi's also done a wonderful job of raising a child on her own," Sam said. "And Jenna's a great kid. She looks after Will sometimes when our nanny has a day off. He adores her."

Okay, he could be dense at times but he knew where this conversation was going.

"I can see that," he said. Molly and Martha were already crazy about Kristi and her daughter. And unless he admitted he'd screwed up, Sam would continue to sing their praises. "I overreacted to something this afternoon. I owe them an apology."

Sam used her hammer to knock the last stubborn shelf out of place, stuck it back in her tool belt and handed the board to him. "If you don't mind taking these shelves out to the garage, I'll get started on this wallpaper." Judging by her satisfied smile, he'd said everything she wanted to hear and the conversation was over.

NATE'S GARAGE DOOR was open and Kristi could see him inside when she returned from the mall. There was no sign of the girls or Sam. A good thing, because it would give them a chance to talk in private.

She walked in, and his grim smile suggested he wanted to talk to her, too. "Hi."

"Hi," she said. "Are those the bookshelves from your office?"

"They are. I thought I'd store them here till I figure out what to do with them. Sam helped me take them apart and now she's inside pulling down the wallpaper."

And probably grumbling about it, knowing Sam. "What are the girls doing?"

"Watching a DVD."

"Good. I was hoping we'd have a chance to talk."

"Me, too." He separated a couple of white plastic lawn chairs and offered her one. They sat facing each other, sandwiched between his SUV and the workbench that ran the length of one wall.

"I'm really sorry about the way I reacted to Jenna putting makeup on the girls. She didn't do anything wrong, and I was completely out of line. I hope you'll tell her that."

"Thank you, I will. But I think you should speak to her yourself."

"I will. Tomorrow before we go to my family's place." *If she'll agree to go.* "I'll be sure to tell her that when I get home."

"Thanks. If there's anything I can do to make it up to her…"

Poor guy. He really did feel badly about what had happened. "Well, she's been begging me to buy her an iPhone," she said, hoping to lighten his mood.

His eyebrows went up a notch.

Kristi laughed. "That was supposed to be a joke."

That got her a smile, and he seemed to relax a little. "It would serve me right if it wasn't."

"Jenna's feathers were a little ruffled but she'll get over it. If you don't mind me asking, and feel free to tell me to mind my own business if you do, what made you so angry? The girls have loads of dress-up clothes. I understand why parents don't want little girls wearing makeup, but they were just playing and it washes off."

He ran a hand through his hair, the way he did when he was carefully choosing his words. She resisted the urge to smooth it out for him. "It's kind of a long story," he said.

"I have time."

"I told you about Heather's mother, how she did everything she could to save Heather's life."

A knot formed in Kristi's stomach as she wondered where this was going.

"Losing Heather was hard on everyone, but for Alice…"

He sighed. "She didn't cope well. She blamed me. Still does, I think."

"What? Why? That's crazy."

"Not to her. If it wasn't for the pregnancy, Heather would still be alive. And since I'm the one who got her pregnant, I'm the one who caused her death."

"Oh, Nate. I understand that grief hits people hard, but you said your wife had already lost one kidney. Anything could have happened."

"Yeah, well, Alice doesn't see it that way."

"How is she with Molly and Martha? Surely she doesn't take it out on them."

"Oh, no. Pretty much the opposite. She dotes on them and she's constantly buying toys and clothes."

Hence the overabundance of things in the girls' bedroom.

"Her latest thing is wanting to enter them in a children's beauty pageant."

So that was it. The girls had been pretending to be beauty queens, and the disgust in his voice told her exactly what he thought of pageants. "And I gather that's not what you want?"

"They're four years old. What do they need with a beauty pageant?" He looked at her as though he couldn't believe she had asked. "Would you have put your daughter in one? Did you?"

"No, of course not. I agree with you. Lots of parents think it's the right thing to do for their kids, though."

"Alice isn't the parent here. She has no business pushing this on us."

"Did you tell her that?"

"I told her I didn't think it was a good idea."

Not a good idea? Clearly it was the worst idea Nate

had ever heard. Kristi understood why he was reluctant to stand up to the woman, but he had to do it.

She covered his hands with hers. "Again, this is none of my business, but your mother-in-law sounds like the kind of woman who doesn't like to take no for an answer. So if you don't tell her no, she sure isn't going to hear it."

"You're right, of course. I've been hoping that if I let it slide, we would miss the entry deadline and then it wouldn't be an issue."

He was a smart man, so he couldn't possibly believe that. And it was kind of sweet that he didn't want to offend the girls' grandmother, even though Kristi had a hunch he mostly wanted to avoid a confrontation. "If she doesn't get her way with this, is she likely to back off? If she really believes the pageant is a good idea, she'll just try again next year."

He turned his hands over and curled his fingers around hers. "You're right. She will, and if it's not the pageant, she'll come up with something else."

"So you're going to talk to her?"

He gave a reluctant nod. "I'm not looking forward to it but you're right. I don't have a choice."

"Can I offer one more suggestion?" She didn't want to seem like yet another person who was meddling in his life, but he could do with a little encouragement.

"Of course."

"Don't let this just be about the pageant. Make it about your family—you and your daughters. Your mother-in-law needs to know that you're open to her suggestions, but in the end, you're the one who makes the decisions about what's best for them."

She held her breath, not sure how he would react. For a few seconds he didn't, then he squeezed her hands and gave her a smile that heated up her insides. "I don't suppose you'd like to talk to her," he said with a shallow laugh.

She laughed, too. "No way. I'm scared of her, and I haven't even met her."

Nate slid his hands up her arms, making her shiver a little. "That makes two of us. But I will do it."

They sat, knee to knee, gazes locked. His hands stopped at her shoulders, and he pulled her closer as he leaned in. His kiss was easy and light, unexpected and welcome.

"Thank you." The words against her lips were as soft as a whisper.

"You're welcome."

"I should go in and check on the girls."

"And I should get back to work."

Neither of them wanted to break the connection, though.

"It's too bad this thing we've got going on here isn't real," he said. "We'd make a great team."

She should be hearing alarm bells right now, but instead her heart was doing cartwheels in her chest. She wasn't looking for a team, she was used to doing things for herself. So where were those damn bells, and why weren't they ringing?

Chapter Nine

On Sunday morning, Nate put Gemmy in the backyard, strapped the girls into their car seats in the backseat of the SUV and drove to Kristi's place. To his relief, she had accepted his apology and agreed to keep their "date" to his sister's birthday brunch. Now he just needed to apologize to Jenna and they'd be good.

Kristi's town house complex was well cared for and located in a good neighborhood. He easily found her unit and pulled into the space next to her minivan.

"Girls, I want you to stay buckled up and wait in the car, okay? I'll ring the bell and let Kristi know we're here, then I'll come back and wait with you.

"No!" the girls chorused from the backseat.

"I want to see Jenna's room!"

"I want to play with Herc!"

"There's no time to play with Hercules this morning. You can play with him next time Kristi brings him to our place." He got out and closed the door on any further protest.

Kristi's front entrance was flanked by a pair of cedar planters filled with petunias that badly needed deadheading. He stuck a finger in the soil. And water. The painted metal Home Sweet Home sign on the front door was either old, or made to look old. Either way, it was a nice touch.

He pressed the button for the bell and Hercules started to bark. The yipping grew louder, and Nate could hear Kristi shushing the dog. She was all smiles when she opened the door, the overexcited little dog wriggling in her arms.

"Hi," he said.

"Hi. We're running a little behind, but we're almost ready."

He'd been half expecting that. "Anything I can do to help?"

"Can you take your sister's gift and this box of cup-cakes out to your car?" She indicated the items sitting on the bench inside the narrow entryway. "Jenna?" she called upstairs. "Nate's here. Are you ready to go?"

"Yeah, yeah, yeah. I'll be down in a second," she yelled back, but didn't sound convincing.

"I'll get this little guy settled in his crate and be right back."

"No problem." Nate stepped inside, picked up the items on the bench and took a hasty look around. The three wicker baskets lined up under the bench had name tags on them, one for each resident, including the dog.

Given what Kristi did for a living, he had expected her home to be ultraorganized, but the living room looked lived in. The white furniture was cozy and inviting. Ev-erything else in the room, from the accent cushions to the prints on the walls, was splashed with color—pink and red and orange. The overall effect was bright and fresh and feminine, and it was Kristi to a tee.

Listen to you, he thought as he carried the gift and the cake box outside and stowed them securely in the back of his SUV. *You've turned into a regular Martha Stewart.*

His daughters' excited voices filled the car. "Jenna!"

Kristi's daughter stood in the doorway, wearing a pair

of narrow-legged black jeans, a baggy white T-shirt with an indistinguishable black print on the front and a sullen expression. The long red scarf looped several times around her neck matched the red canvas runners on her feet. Her hair hung in two loose braids, and he'd swear she had on even more eye makeup than ever. She was not happy, and a guy didn't need to be a rocket scientist to figure out he was the source of her displeasure.

So much for Kristi saying she would talk to her and smooth things over. Or maybe there *had* been talking, just no smoothing. And right now, holding the car door open for the reluctant daughter of the woman he was fake dating, he didn't care for either scenario.

"I hope you don't mind riding in the back with the twins," he said.

She shrugged and got in without making eye contact, then bestowed a bright smile on the girls. "Aw, look at you guys. I love your outfits."

They had insisted on wearing the fussy, frilly dresses Alice and Fred had given them for their birthday.

"No fair!" Martha said. "I want Jenna beside me."

"No! She's aside me." At least Molly left off her trademark nya-nya-nya-nya-nya.

"You can trade places on the way home," Jenna said. "That way I get to sit beside both of you."

"That's a good idea," Nate said.

Jenna ignored him and shut the door, not quite firmly enough for him to say she slammed it but darned close.

He should have apologized to her yesterday but she'd stormed out, and then by the time he'd cooled off, she was gone. Now she wasn't going to make this easy for him, and who could blame her?

He was debating whether to go back inside or wait for

Kristi by the car when she hurried out of the house and locked the door behind her.

God, she looked good. Her navy pants, cropped just below the knee, kept those great gams in full view. Her white top and bright yellow jacket were neither too casual nor overly dressy. Perfect for a family brunch.

"How was Jenna?" she asked, keeping her voice low.

"Not happy."

"I'm sorry about that. I'll talk to her again."

So, she had tried.

"I'll talk to her." At least he would try. "I need to apologize, and that's not something you can do for me."

Kristi looked unconvinced. "I'm sorry I kept you waiting. I was working on something for your girls' bedroom and lost track of time."

"No problem." She was worth the wait. He opened the door for her, appreciating the graceful way she slid in.

He was lucky that things were okay between him and Kristi. Now he had to come up with a plan to win Jenna over.

AT HIS PARENTS' PLACE, Britt met them at the front door and chaos reigned for several minutes. She gushed over everyone's gifts, declaring "oh, you shouldn't have" without being even a little bit convincing. Molly and Martha, excited to demonstrate the swirliness of their party dresses and shamelessly encouraged by their aunt, twirled until they fell into a giggling heap.

Kristi introduced Jenna, who was still giving him the cold shoulder but instantly warmed to his sister's compliment on her T-shirt. Turns out the baggy garment with the indiscernible print on the front was, in fact, the work of a hip young Seattle designer, and everybody who was anybody either had one or wanted to have one.

"I'll take these into the kitchen," he said, carefully balancing the large plastic box filled with Kristi's cupcakes.

"I can take them," Kristi said.

"No, you stay here with my sister and the girls." He followed the scent of coffee and bacon and his mother's amazing pastry into the kitchen, deciding he'd go back out after introductions, birthday greetings, dress twirling and gushy compliments about everyone's fashion sense dropped from earsplittingly loud to something a little more conversational.

"Nathan, sorry I didn't meet you and Kristi at the door. I was whipping cream and I didn't want to leave it."

"No problem, Mom." He set the box on the counter and kissed her cheek. "You look wonderful."

"Thank you. What's in the container?"

"Kristi's cupcakes. They're really good."

"You've already sampled her cupcakes?"

He studied her face, expecting a sassy smile to accompany that remark. Instead, she opened the container. "Wow. These are really something."

"I know. She brought some for the girls, sort of a reward for clearing out their bedroom, and they loved them."

His mother covered a tray of deviled eggs with plastic wrap and slid it into the fridge. "She runs a business, sews her own clothes, decorates cakes…she sounds like a keeper."

"Mom…please." He didn't want to go there.

"I'm just saying…"

"I know you are, but don't start. Not today, okay?"

"Is something wrong?" Her concern was genuine, and it touched him.

"Everything's fine. Her daughter and I had a little run-in yesterday, and she's not very happy with me right now." He wasn't looking for sympathy or advice, he just wanted to explain the situation up front. Nothing got past his mother, and Jenna's frosty demeanor was not subtle so she wouldn't miss it.

"Blended families require a big adjustment. They take work," she said. "And patience." She rinsed a mixing spoon and put it in the dishwasher. "Can you get me a clean towel, please?"

He pulled one from a drawer and passed it to her. Blended families? Geez, where did that come from? This wasn't even a real date, but then she didn't know that.

"We just met. Talking about families is a little premature." Raising a pair of four-year-olds was hard enough. He wasn't ready for a teenager.

"Don't worry," she said, filling the coffeepot with cold water. "I would never say anything in front of Kristi and her daughter, but I have a good feeling about this. All I'm saying is that it's going to take work." She measured ground coffee into the basket.

Time to change the subject, he decided. If Kristi or, heaven forbid, Jenna were to walk into the kitchen right now, he didn't want them to overhear this conversation. Ditto for his sister. His mother might not say anything to Kristi, but Britt wasn't known for her restraint.

"Would you like some help?" he asked.

"Since it's such a beautiful day, I thought I would serve brunch in the sunroom. The table's already set, but you can start carrying the salads out there."

"You made more than one salad?"

"I made four."

"Four salads?"

"That's right. I always make potato salad for your father—it's his favorite. I made a green salad for Britt because it's swimsuit season and she's watching her weight. And it is her birthday, after all. There's also the macaroni salad that Molly and Martha like so much, the one with ham in it. I wasn't sure if Kristi and Jenna would care for any of those, so I whipped up a fruit salad, as well."

Nate opened the fridge. The four huge salads seemed like way too much for eight people, but he kept that thought to himself. "What's in the oven?" he asked, setting the bowls on the counter.

"Quiches. Your father has to watch his cholesterol, but since it's a special occasion, I promised I'd make quiche lorraines for him."

For most of his life Nate had taken his parents' easy, comfortable relationship for granted. It was only in the past few years that he'd realized they worked at it, not because they had to but because they wanted to, and after all these years they were still very much in love.

"The salad servers are in the second drawer, next to the stove," his mother said. "I also made tomato and basil quiches, in case Kristi and her daughter are vegetarian."

He peeked through the oven door as he opened the drawer. Four quiches. Enough food to feed a small army, as usual. He peeled plastic wrap off the salad bowls, stuck a serving spoon into each and carried two of them into the sunroom.

The table was set with white china and crisp-looking green linens, a centerpiece of freshly cut flowers from his mother's garden and his grandmother's silver candelabras, which had been polished till they sparkled. He knew his mother well enough to realize she'd set the table last night, but he was also certain she'd been up since before dawn to make sure Britt had a special day.

He set the salads on the sideboard and met Kristi on his way back to the kitchen. She was carrying the other two salads.

"Your mother said you were out here."

He took one of the bowls from her, liking the feel of her hand against his as she let it go.

"Thanks," she said after the transfer was made. "Where should I put the fruit salad?"

"Over there with the others."

"Wow. That's a lot of salads."

"This is just the beginning," he said. "There's also a tray of deviled eggs and umpteen quiches. Then there'll be a birthday cake, and I'm sure dessert won't stop there because my mother was whipping cream when we arrived." So much for his father's arteries.

She laughed at that. "Oh, my goodness. Maybe I shouldn't have brought the cupcakes."

"Mom was impressed that you made them." He touched the small of her back on their return to the kitchen, and he leaned in to whisper, "She says you're a keeper."

Kristi stopped walking. "She said that?"

"She did." Although, after asking his mother not to say anything to Kristi, he had no idea why he was telling her.

"Well, I'm flattered. What did you say?"

"Oh, don't worry. I downplayed it as much as I could. Reminded her that we'd just met and we're taking things slow."

A flirty little smile tugged at the corners of her mouth. "Right. Good answer."

She was thinking about their Friday-night kiss. And their Saturday-afternoon kiss. That was a lot of kissing for two people who'd just met and were going slow.

"I don't want her to get the wrong idea," he said. "We don't want to go down that road." That was such a contradiction, given that he was pretty far down the wrong road himself.

"But we don't want her to get the *right* idea, either."

"The right idea?"

She leaned close, and her whisper caressed his ear. "That we're not really dating at all."

For a few seconds he was only aware of his physical reaction to her warm breath against his skin.

"All right, you two. Get a room."

He'd been so caught up with Kristi, he hadn't seen Britt walking toward them with the deviled eggs. Had she heard what Kristi said? Judging by her approving grin, she had not.

Kristi pulled away, her face flushed.

"God, you guys are cute." Britt winked as she breezed by. "Kristi, my mom dug out her cupcake stand for you."

"She has a cupcake stand?"

"Actually, she has two. Crate & Barrel has nothing on our mother. Right, Nate?"

What could he say? He didn't want to talk about cupcakes or their mother's extremely well-equipped home. He wanted everyone to go away. He wanted Kristi to whisper something, anything, in his ear again. It didn't even have to be real words.

"Right," he said instead. "Come on. I'll give you a hand."

Kristi let him guide her down the hallway and into his mother's kitchen.

You can do this, he told himself. *You're a smart guy.* He would get through this phoney date, he would figure out a way to get Jenna on his side and he would ask Kristi out on an actual date. No kids, no dogs, no family. Just the two of them, for real.

THE BRUNCH WAS elegantly simple, very much like Nate's mother, Kristi thought. Her family's events tended to be a little more freewheeling and raucous, which now had her second-guessing the wisdom of inviting him to Aunt

Wanda and Uncle Ted's next weekend. The Fourth of July festivities would take place in their backyard and every year it was the same, with Uncle Ted presiding over the barbecue and her cousin Bart in charge of keeping the cooler stocked with soft drinks and beer. Aunt Wanda would provide a mountain of sweet, buttered corn on the cob, Kristi's mom would bring coleslaw and Kristi would bake a double batch of her grandmother's cupcakes, a family favorite that only she had ever learned to make.

It was always fun, but very different from brunch with Nate's family. His parents sat at either end of the table. His mother had seated Jenna between the twins, and across from them Nate sat between Kristi and Britt.

This arrangement put Nate and Jenna directly across the table from one another, and by the middle of the meal her daughter had yet to look directly at him. On the one hand, Kristi didn't blame her for being annoyed with Nate. On the other, her standoffishness was becoming tiresome. Nate was sorry he'd overreacted, and last night Kristi had pleaded his case. Jenna was having none of it, which, hormonal teenager aside, was out of character for her.

Kristi couldn't tell if anyone else noticed her frostiness. And to her daughter's credit, she good-naturedly helped Molly and Martha unfold their napkins and even cut their quiches into manageable bite-size pieces. She politely answered Helen's and Roger's questions about her friends and her favorite subjects at school, and she was clearly captivated by Britt's vivaciousness. On the one occasion that Nate had addressed a comment directly to her, she had pretended not to hear and he had wisely let it go.

"Would anyone like more salad or quiche before I clear the table for dessert?" Helen asked.

Kristi quickly slid her chair back from the table. "Let me help."

"Certainly not. You sit and chat with Britt. Pour yourself another mimosa if you'd like."

"I'd like one," Britt said. "It's not every day a girl turns thirty, and I'm not driving." She filled her champagne flute and reached for Kristi's.

"Just half a glass, please."

Britt poured a generous half. "Nate? More for you?"

"I'll pass, thanks. I am driving."

Helen nodded approvingly. "Good plan. Besides, I thought I would ask you and Jenna to give me a hand clearing away the dishes so I can serve dessert."

"Birthday cake!" Molly shouted.

"Candles!"

Nate shushed them. "Martha, Molly. Inside voices, please."

Kristi connected with Jenna's wary look and gave her an encouraging smile, wondering as she did if Helen's request was as innocent as it sounded.

Jenna got up and flipped her scarf over her shoulder. "What would you like me to do?"

"I'll clear the table if you and Nate will take the salad bowls into the kitchen. He'll show you where I keep the containers for leftovers."

Nate leaned close and gave Kristi's shoulder a gentle squeeze as he got up from the table. "Wish me luck." Fortunately no one else could hear over the girls' clamoring to help.

"I can carry stuff," Martha said.

Molly's fork clattered onto her plate. "Me, too."

"Thank you, but I have a special job for the two of you," their grandmother said.

"What?" they chorused. "What?"

"See that basket of presents over there by the door? How would the two of you like to carry them over to the table and put them next to your aunt Britt? Then she can open them right after we have cake."

While Britt checked her iPhone for messages and Roger stepped outside to stretch his legs and "make room for dessert," Kristi sipped her mimosa and watched Helen slowly and carefully stack the plates. She appeared to be taking her time so she could monitor her granddaughters as they ferried Britt's gifts from the basket to the table, but Kristi wasn't buying it. She had a pretty good hunch that Helen knew something was amiss between Nate and Jenna, and she'd intentionally sent them to the kitchen so they could work out their differences.

Would they, or would Helen's plan make matters worse?

Kristi kept an ear tuned to the hallway that led to the kitchen, but heard nothing. How long did it take to pack up a couple of salads?

"Good job, girls. You're both such great helpers, and I really like how you made sure the cards and gifts stayed together. Thank you."

Helen bent and put an arm around each child. Martha rested her head against her grandmother's thigh and popped her thumb in her mouth, but Molly only stayed for a second before bouncing back around the table and leaning next to her aunt.

"Aunt Britt?"

"Yes, Molly?"

"Do you need help opening your presents?"

"I definitely will. Any chance you and Martha would be interested?"

"Yes!"

Martha continued to cling to her grandmother, but she nodded vigorously.

Helen smoothed the little girl's hair and helped her back into her chair, then slowly gathered up the cutlery.

She's definitely killing time, Kristi thought.

Finally Helen picked up the dishes. "I'll take these into the kitchen and see how Nate and Jenna are getting along."

And there it was. She had picked up on Jenna's resentment, or maybe Nate had said something to her, and she was giving them a chance to work out their differences. Kristi hoped her plan didn't backfire.

NATE KNEW WHY his mother had sent him and Jenna into the kitchen together. He had deliberately not told her why Jenna was angry with him, but his mother was one astute woman. And because she thought he and Kristi were embarking on a serious relationship, she was taking it upon herself to fix things. Now it was up to him to find the right thing to say to Jenna so he didn't make matters worse.

He found four empty containers in the pantry and set them on the counter.

"Here you go. We can put the leftovers in these."

She didn't say anything as she scooped macaroni salad from the bowl into the plastic container. She didn't have to. The thump of the spoon against plastic spoke volumes.

"Jenna, I'm sorry about yesterday. I overreacted—"

Thump, thump, thump.

"Okay. I was completely out of line. I was…well, let's face it…I acted like an ass, and I'm sorry."

That worked. He could tell she wanted to smile but wasn't giving in to the urge.

"My mom wouldn't be happy to hear you swearing."

"I'm sure she wouldn't. I'll apologize to her, too."

For the first time that day, she made direct eye contact. "I didn't do anything wrong. Even my mom said so."

"She's right. After you went to the mall with your friends, she told me she would talk to you." Apparently that conversation had not gone well.

Jenna crossed her arms. "Your kids wanted to play dress-up and I thought it would be fun for them to do makeup, too. We were just playing. There's nothing wrong with that."

From her perspective, he could see that was true. From his, with a mother-in-law who wanted to primp his daughters into a pair of pageant princesses, it had been a red flag. But that had nothing to do with Jenna, and he'd had no business losing his temper with her.

"You're right. There was nothing wrong with it. It's just that fathers…" As soon as the words were out, he realized that talking about fathers with a rebellious girl who didn't have one was venturing into dangerous territory. "Fathers can be clueless when it comes to stuff like this."

She seemed to relax a little.

"Even though Molly and Martha want to grow up and try new things, I guess I want them to stay the way they are." He thought about telling her that if his girls were as great as she was when they were her age, he'd consider himself lucky. But that was a dumb idea. Jenna was way too smart to be won over by sugarcoated compliments.

"What I'm saying is that this is my problem, not yours. I had no right to take it out on you, and I'm sorry."

She unfolded her arms and went back to work on the salad. He wasn't sure if they were okay or not, but he hoped this was her way of letting him know they were.

"My mom hardly ever goes on dates."

He hadn't expected the conversation to turn on a dime, and he was totally unprepared for this new revelation. Telling her that he and her mother technically weren't dating would be the wrong thing to say, but what was the right thing? He had absolutely no idea.

"Is that so?" The question sounded lame but it was the best he could do.

"She wants everyone to think it's on account of my dad ditching us when I was little, but it's mostly because she wants to set an example for me."

Those were almost the exact words Kristi herself had used when she had explained the deadbeat reference. Did she realize that her daughter knew what was motivating her? Somehow he didn't think she did.

"Do you and your mom talk about those things?"

"Not really, but I hear stuff and see stuff."

Good to know. "How do you feel about her not dating?" He asked because he genuinely wanted to know. He just wished he could have found a way to do it without sounding like a psychologist on a TV talk show.

Jenna shrugged. "I don't know. I just want her to be happy, I guess."

"Do you think she is?"

She faced him again. "Yeah, I do. She's a pretty cool mom…"

How many teenagers would admit to thinking something like that?

But Jenna wasn't finished. "And I'd be really pissed if anybody did anything to hurt her."

Bingo. Now they were getting somewhere. She resented his misdirected anger over the makeup fiasco—and who could blame her?—but her real resentment ran a lot deeper.

A few minutes ago their conversation had been well outside his comfort zone. This new twist had him scrambling. What was the right thing to say here? To hell with the right thing—he couldn't think of *anything* to say.

He remembered one time back in his senior year in high school, he had gone to a girl's home to pick her up, and her father had outlined the consequences for any boy who did anything to his daughter. It hadn't even been a date, as he recalled. They were going to a chemistry study group. Then there had been numerous lectures from his own father. Not "the talk" in the sense that Kristi had referred to the other night, but more of a "be a gentleman" kind of thing. He'd managed to wait till he was almost finished grad school before getting his girlfriend pregnant, and by then he knew well enough what doing the right thing meant.

That's not what Jenna meant, though. Or he hoped it wasn't. She would be "pissed" if someone hurt her mom in the emotional sense. She was also enjoying being in control of the situation, having turned the tables on him, and she was waiting for him to respond.

"Ah…" He hated to think what shade of red his face had turned. "I would never…not intentionally…ever do anything to hurt your mother."

Not what she wanted to hear, apparently.

What else could he say? He and Kristi had a business relationship, and together they'd hatched this plan to be each other's plus-one as a way to avoid the awkward setups their families kept arranging for them. This was supposed to be simple, straightforward, easy. How had it become so complicated, so fast?

It became complicated when he kissed her, which was right around the time he'd figured out that he'd like their arrangement to be more than a matter of convenience. That much he could acknowledge, even to Jenna, because it was true. And if she repeated it to Kristi, which he strongly suspected she would, it would sound as though he was covering up the fake dating scenario by making it sound real.

"Your mom and I are just getting to know each other, and right now neither of us has a clue where this is headed or how the future's going to look. We're taking it slow." Kristi had laughed when he'd said that earlier. Lucky for him, Jenna seemed to accept it at face value.

"Good." She went to work on the last salad bowl—no thumping this time—while he stowed the other containers in the fridge.

For another couple of minutes they worked in comfortable silence while she rinsed the bowls and he loaded them in the dishwasher.

On their way back to the sunroom they passed his mother, carrying a stack of plates and cutlery.

"Everything okay?" she asked.

"Everything's fine," he said. "Do you need a hand with anything else?"

"You go join the others, and let your father know he should come in for dessert. Jenna, would you mind helping me? You can bring in your mom's cupcakes."

Kristi gave him a questioning look when he joined her at the table.

"Everything okay?" It was the same question his mother had asked, right down to the subtext.

He seated himself and reached for Kristi's hand beneath the table, glad that for the moment Molly and Martha were outside with their grandfather and Britt was occupied with her phone.

"Better than okay."

Her smile was probably meant to convey *thank you*. What he saw was a mouth he desperately wanted to kiss, a face he wanted to look at over and over again and a woman who deserved so much more than a fake relationship.

Chapter Ten

Every Monday morning Kristi met Sam and Claire at Ready Set Sold's downtown office, dropped off the past week's receipts and other paperwork, and then the three of them held their weekly business meeting over coffee at a café down the block. This morning, in spite of her best intentions, she was running a little late. Sam and Claire were already at the coffee shop, and Marlie, their office manager, was talking into her headset, her long acrylic nails clacking on her keyboard.

Today the nails were purple with silver glitter to match her purple skirt and complement a snug-fitting cream-colored sweater that was lavishly bedazzled with rhinestones. Her hair was big, as were her other assets, including the engagement ring on her left hand. Her boyfriend, Thomas, had proposed last winter but appeared to be in no hurry to set a date.

"Good morning, angel," she said when she was off the phone. "The other two have already gone for coffee." Her nickname, Marlie, was short for Marline. She referred to her three employers as "Marlie's angels," and they loved her for it.

"I know. Claire just sent me a text message." Kristi pulled a manila envelope out of her bag. "These are my receipts. I'm afraid I didn't have time to sort them for you."

"Did you write the clients' names on them?"

"These are all for the Anderson house. I finished there last week, so this should be it for that project."

Marlie reached for the envelope. "Hand them over. I'll sort them."

"You will?" Kristi blew her a kiss. "You're my favorite office manager in the whole world."

"I understand you've taken on an interesting new client." Her emphasis on the word *interesting* told Kristi that Sam or Claire, possibly both, had told her about Nate. She knew her partners well enough to know they wouldn't tell Marlie the whole story.

Kristi decided to play along. "Very interesting. Of all the houses I've worked on, this is definitely my favorite so far."

"And the owner?"

Ditto. "He's..."

"Sam says he's a real catch."

Kristi laughed. "Okay, Sam did *not* say that." Sam never said things like that.

"You're right, but she didn't have to. Besides, Claire showed me his picture." The phone rang, and Marlie clicked a button on her headset. "Ready Set Sold. How may I help you?"

Kristi took advantage of the distraction and slipped into the tiny office she shared with her two partners. Shortly after they opened the business, they'd found space on the second floor of an old building near Pioneer Square. The small reception area was Marlie's domain. It led to an even smaller office that Kristi technically shared with her two business partners. Kristi tended to work at home and out of her minivan because it meant she could spend more time with Jenna, and Sam ran the construction end of the business out of the ancient delivery truck she had converted into a mobile workshop.

Claire used the office more than either of them, especially to meet with clients, and the space was organized accordingly. The glass-topped desk with dark espresso-colored legs had been Kristi's idea because it made the small room feel more open. The surface, completely free of fingerprints and clutter, was all Claire's doing.

On the back wall above a narrow credenza were three framed photographs that showcased some of their recent projects. Kristi changed them every month, and next week she'd be adding new ones. Right now the display consisted of a cedar deck Sam had recently refurbished on the back of a home overlooking Lake Union, a one-and-a-half-story Tudor in Montlake with Claire's Sold sign in the front yard and a before-and-after montage of a handyman's workbench that Kristi had organized.

Her phone buzzed. Another text message from Claire, wondering when she would join them. She grabbed her bag and waved at Marlie as she retraced her steps through the front office, texting a hasty I'm on my way!

THE HOUSE FELT quiet, almost too quiet. Nate set his laptop on the peninsula and turned it on. Half an hour ago his mother had picked up the girls and they were spending the day at the zoo and having dinner at their favorite fast-food restaurant. They wouldn't be home until bedtime.

Kristi had a meeting with her business partners this morning, and then she was going shopping for "storage solutions" that would help him keep the house organized. He probably could have found a reason to go with her, but as much as he enjoyed spending time with her, he didn't care for shopping. Her business partner, Sam, would arrive midmorning to finish painting. She had also made arrangements for someone to give him an estimate on putting a fence around the swimming pool. He walked to the patio doors and gazed out at the yard where Gemmy lay sprawled in the sun.

He and Heather had loved the idea of having a pool, spending time out there with the girls. It had been one of the deciding factors when they bought the house, right after they got married, but they had never used it. By the time they moved in, Heather's health was deteriorating. After the girls were born, he could barely keep his head above water in the figurative sense. With the demands of his family and launching his career at the university, there had been no time for relaxation. By the next summer Heather was very sick, and with two toddlers, the pool had been nothing more than a safety hazard. He'd had it drained and the cover installed, and it had been like that ever since.

For the past two years, fixing up the pool had been relegated to the list of things it would be nice to do…someday. For now, he had two little girls who depended on him for everything. Three meals a day, clean clothes, bedtime stories. Everything he had to do to live up to his promise to Heather, to love the girls enough for both of them. In between he prepared lectures, graded papers, carried out research projects and sat on faculty committees.

Give your head a shake, man. He had a rare day to himself and he had work to do. He shouldn't be dredging up the past. After being in a holding pattern for the past two years, his life was changing. And all because of Kristi. He was disappointed she wouldn't be here today. If she was, he might have an easier time settling down to work. Or he'd be completely distracted.

He turned away from the window, switched on his computer and forced himself to take a seat. One thing was certain. Kristi's being here couldn't be any more distracting than her not being here. He opened the document containing the paper he was working on and stared at the screen. He was so relieved when the phone rang that he grabbed it and answered without checking the call display.

"Nate, it's Alice. I've been expecting you to call."

He knew that, and in spite of the talk he'd had with Kristi on the weekend, he had been reluctant to contact Alice.

"Sorry. It's been pretty hectic around here, with all the renovations going on, and I had some family things this weekend."

"I see."

"We celebrated my sister's thirtieth birthday." The last thing he needed was for Alice to feel snubbed.

"That's nice," she said, without sounding as though she meant it. "I'm calling to see if you've filled out those entry forms yet."

"Not yet. Like I said, we've been busy."

"The entry deadline is next week. We don't have much time."

"I've been meaning to talk to you about that. I appreciate you thinking of the girls, but I've decided not to enter them. It's just not right for us." He stopped talking before he added that there was no way in hell his daughters were being paraded around in public like a pair of little divas.

There was a long silence. "I wish you'd said something sooner. I had those head shots taken. Their dresses have been picked out."

He held the phone away from his ear and stared at it for a few seconds. *No one asked you to do any of those things.* "I'm sorry you went to all that effort. Next time something comes up, I won't take so long to make a decision."

"Fine." Her tone implied she was anything but. "What are the girls doing this morning? Can I talk to them?"

"Sorry, Alice. They're not here. My parents picked them up half an hour ago. They're spending the day at the zoo."

"Oh. All right, then." As usual, she didn't mind letting him know she was disappointed.

"We'll call you before bedtime so they can say goodnight."

"That gives me and Fred something to look forward to."

If Fred had ever had an opinion about anything, the poor man had given up expressing it years ago. Now he wouldn't dare look forward to something unless his wife told him to.

"Great. We'll talk to you then."

He set the phone on the counter, then let out a whoop and punched the air. He'd done it! Kristi would be so proud of him. He'd stood up to Alice, said no to the pageant, and it had been way easier than he ever would have imagined. Why hadn't he done this a long time ago? He knew the answer.

Half an hour after saying goodbye to Heather for the last time, he'd stood in the hospital corridor with Alice and Fred. He had probably been exhausted, no doubt worried as hell about how his future as a single father would unfold, but all he remembered about that day was the overwhelming numbness.

And then there was Alice, in his face, her emotions raw and roiling on the surface.

"How could you do this to her? My daughter would still be alive if it weren't for those babies."

Those babies—his two innocent darling girls, the loves of his and Heather's lives—were with his family. Unbeknownst to them, their lives had changed forever, and now they had a grandmother who resented their very existence.

And since their existence was his doing, she resented him, too. He had a vague recollection of Fred hovering silently in the background, saying nothing as always. He'd had little more than disdain for his father-in-law in those early days after Heather died. Now he sympathized with the man.

Heather had been their only child, and when she was diagnosed with type 1 diabetes at age seven, keeping her healthy had become Alice's sole purpose in life. Not long after he and Heather met, she had described how her mother had become overprotective, constantly worrying and monitoring her blood sugar, preventing her from doing many of the things kids did—having dinner at a friend's house, going to sleepovers, even playing sports. Heather had been strong-willed and determined, and she had rebelled. To some degree, her rebellion led to complications, and by the time she was in her late teens she'd had a kidney removed.

Having a baby would be risky—she'd known that—and when they did find out the twins were on the way, Alice had wanted the pregnancy terminated. Heather dug in her heels and insisted on going through with it, and Nate had been caught in the middle, not knowing whose side to be on, not wanting to have to choose.

Although they hadn't planned to have a family—hell, they hadn't even planned to get married at that point— he'd always assumed he'd have one someday. A career, a wife, a house, a couple of kids, a dog…that's what he'd grown up expecting to have.

He'd felt trapped and guilty and that guilt had been compounded by his mother-in-law after Heather's death. But then a month after the funeral she'd rung his doorbell and insinuated herself back into Nate's and his daughters' lives. There had been no explanation, no apology, and she'd been around ever since, lavishing the girls with expensive gifts and sending him on a guilt trip every chance she got.

Today, after two years, he'd finally put a stop to it. He couldn't wait to tell Kristi. He sat down at his computer, but instead he was thinking about all the ways he'd like to thank her.

KRISTI DASHED INTO the coffee shop and joined Sam and Claire at their usual table in the back corner. "Sorry I'm late."

"You're always late," Sam said. She was dressed in her usual blue jeans and work shirt, and her coffee cup was already half-empty.

"Funny. I meant later than usual. I can't seem to get—"

"Organized?" Claire asked. Her navy jacket over a crisp white blouse suggested she'd be showing properties to prospective buyers that morning.

"Also funny. I was going to say focused."

Sam and Claire exchanged a look.

"Don't start," Kristi said. "This has nothing to do with Nate." They wouldn't believe her, and why should they when she couldn't even convince herself?

"We'll talk about that later." Claire ran a finger across her iPad screen and perused her list. "Let's get started."

When they'd first formed their partnership, they had established one simple rule for their meetings. Business first, then, if there was time, they could chat about personal stuff.

"Thanks for ordering a pot of tea for me." Kristi pulled out her wallet and laptop, handed Claire a pair of ones to cover the purchase and turned on her computer.

Claire tucked the money into her handbag. "So, we

have a couple of projects wrapping up. Where are we with those?"

"New gutters and downspouts installed on the Anderson house," Sam said. "The perimeter drains have been cleaned out, too, so the moisture problems in the basement have been addressed."

"Let's hope so," Kristi said. "That was one of the worst basements I've seen in ages."

"But you should see it now," Sam said to Claire. "This woman worked her magic, convinced the Andersons to replace the carpet with laminate, painted the dark blue walls a nice off-white. You'd never know it was the same place."

"You did most of the work," Kristi reminded her. And as usual she'd done an amazing job.

"You hauled the junk out of there and got rid of it." Sam gave a mock shudder. "All those boxes of musty old magazines. Gross."

Claire shuddered for real. "You both amaze me. I meet with the Anderson family tomorrow. Now that the estate has been settled, we can move forward with the listing." She made some quick notes.

Twenty minutes later brought them to the McTavish house. Kristi's dream home. Nate's place.

Claire looked to Sam first. "What's left for you to do?"

Sam slid her empty coffee cup aside and tapped a pencil against the list on her clipboard. "I primed the office and the kids' bedroom walls on Saturday…while Kristi was out shopping." She winked at Claire.

"I saw that," Kristi said.

They both smiled.

"Got started on the closet organizers and bookcases on Saturday afternoon."

"How does AJ feel about you working so much?" Claire asked.

"I'm building them in my workshop at home and Will was out there with me, so he didn't seem to mind at all." Sam grinned. "Besides, he had a deadline for an article for a business magazine, so he was working, too."

"You have no idea how jealous I am." Claire was the most traditional of the three of them. She longed for a husband, a home in the suburbs with a white picket fence and a family, and in that order. So far she had a soon-to-be ex-husband, an ultramodern penthouse in a downtown condominium and a biological clock that, according to her, ticked so loud it kept her awake at night.

"Don't be jealous," Sam said. "Your time will come when the right guy comes along."

"Like he has for Kristi." Claire gave her hand a warm squeeze. "I'm jealous of you, too. But before we talk about you, we need to wrap up here. What else needs to be done on the McTavish house?"

Kristi opened the file. "Inside, after Sam's finished painting, I'm pretty much down to decluttering and cleaning. That'll take another week or so. Oh, and I'm making curtains for the girls' bedroom—"

Sam and Claire exchanged another look.

"Don't start, you two. I looked for ready-mades online and couldn't find anything, and I can make them for a lot less anyway."

"I think it's very sweet of you," Claire said.

Kristi pressed on. "The exterior of the house is fine but the backyard needs a fair bit of work."

"What about the swimming pool?" Claire asked. "That's one of the main selling features of the house, especially since it's going on the market in the summertime.

"I'm already on it," Sam said. "It was a safety concern with two small children in the home, so it's been empty and kept covered for several years. I discussed the options with Nate when I was there on Saturday, and he's decided to go with glass rails around the pool."

Kristi could picture it perfectly. Molly and Martha in water wings, paddling in the shallow end of the pool. Jenna and her friends hanging out at the other end. She and Nate keeping an eye on all of them from their matching loungers. One big happy…

"Kristi?" Claire's voice snapped her out of the daydream.

"What?"

"We lost you for a minute. I'm wondering how this affects your timeline."

"I was a bit concerned about the pool, especially since the pergola needs work, too. But Sam has a solution."

Sam beamed. "As luck would have it, one of our neighbors owns a company that installs all kinds of railings. Interior, exterior, glass, steel, custom designs, you name it. He and his wife had a baby girl a couple of months ago. Someone in their family gave them a beautiful oak crib and they wanted to add a canopy to it. I had some oak boards left over from the Mill's house we worked on last winter, so I built one for them. They're great neighbors, and since it was basically built from scrap material, I didn't charge them for it. They said if I ever need anything…"

"Perfect," Claire said. "I love it when these things happen."

Kristi patted Sam's hand. "Me, too. Sam's neighbor is meeting her at the house later this morning to give us a quote, and he's said he'll make this a top priority."

"He's a lot like me," Sam said. "He hangs on to everything that's left after an install, and he's pretty sure he has enough material on hand."

Even though Sam had married into money, she was still careful with it. And if she thought something could be used in the future, she didn't throw it away. Ready Set Sold leased a storage locker, and Kristi had lost count of the number of times Sam had dug out something she'd tucked away, saving them a lot of time, and often saving their clients a lot of money.

"That leaves the pergola," Kristi said. "By Wednesday, Nate will be finished collecting data from all those plants and Sam can get started in there. Once they're gone and the plastic cover has been removed, it just needs a coat of stain."

"And then it's a wrap?" Claire asked.

Kristi nodded. They prided themselves on being fast and efficient, but she wasn't ready for this to end.

Claire turned off her iPad and tucked it in her bag. "All right. Now we can get to the good stuff. I want all the details, starting with your first date."

Kristi had a hard time knowing where to begin. Even though she would trust these two women with her life, and even though she knew anything she said went into the vault, she wasn't sure how much to tell them.

Sam leaned on her elbows and grinned. "This could take a while. They've had three dates already."

"We've had *two* dates, and there's not much to tell. Both were with his family, and the second one included our kids. Besides, they're not real dates."

"Ah, but the first 'it's-not-a-real-date' date ended with a kiss." Sensible, practical Claire actually looked a little dreamy eyed.

Kristi's face got warm. Even days later, thinking about that first kiss left her a little breathless.

"The kiss shouldn't have happened," she said. "Seriously, it took us both by surprise. But I wasn't prepared for how easy it is to talk to him."

"Why wouldn't it be?"

"I don't know. For one thing, he's smart."

"So you're saying smart people make lousy conversationalists?" Sam laughed as she said it.

"No, of course not. But he's not your average intelligent guy. He's really smart. He's a university professor, a scientist. He's had stuff published. I saw some of his articles when we were clearing out his office and I couldn't even understand the titles. He's even a member of Mensa." Underneath a pile of books in his office, she'd found a framed certificate with "We're proud of you! Love, Mom & Dad" written on the matte.

"Wow," Claire said.

"Impressive. But doesn't that make him even more interesting?" Sam asked.

"It should, except I'm not smart enough to know what he's talking about."

"Excuse me?" Claire took exception to that. "Don't you dare sell yourself short. You are one of the smartest women I know. Not to mention creative, compassionate and gorgeous. I would kill to have your figure."

"There's nothing wrong with the figure you have," Sam said. "The world would be a boring place if we all looked the same, and if we all had exactly the same interests and ability. Look at us. We're totally different people but we work well together and we're good friends."

True. But as much as Kristi was attracted to Nate and enjoyed being with him, one thing was still niggling at her. Sam had witnessed the scene he'd made over the makeup incident.

"Fine, yes, everything you say is true. But there's still a lot I don't know about him, and I'd be irresponsible if I rushed into anything. Sam, you saw him on Saturday, how angry he got after Jenna put makeup on the twins after they got all dolled up in dress-up clothes."

"Yes, that did seem a little over-the-top."

"Is he still mad?" Claire asked.

"No. He apologized to me on Saturday, and he seemed to smooth things over with Jenna on Sunday." She decided not to mention the children's pageant because she was sure Nate wouldn't want anyone to know about it.

"Dads can be awfully protective when it comes to their daughters," Claire said.

Sam shrugged. "I wouldn't know."

"Neither would I," Kristi said. And maybe that was part of the problem. Nate was so completely different from the fathers she had known. Maybe the good ones were, as Claire suggested, overprotective. "I've known this man for less than a week, and I have more than myself to think about here. Everything I do, every decision I make, it all affects Jenna, too. For me to make the right decisions, I need to take things slow."

"For sure." Claire put an arm around her shoulders and gave a gentle squeeze. "We're not telling you to rush into anything. But I'd hate to see you miss out on a good thing because you're too afraid to take a chance on this guy."

"I do that sometimes, don't I?"

Claire laughed. "Sometimes? Every man you've dated since we've known you has had some major flaw."

Sam laughed, too, and Kristi joined them. "What can I say? My mother and my aunt Wanda introduced me to them. Apparently the world is full of Bernie Halversons."

"Who's Bernie Halverson?" Sam asked.

"The guy who'd be going with me to my aunt and uncle's Fourth of July barbecue if Nate and I hadn't come up with the fake date arrangement."

Claire checked her watch and slid out of her chair. "I'd love to hear more about Nate—Bernie, not so much—

but I'm meeting clients in half an hour. Let's do a quick check-in by conference call at the end of the day, okay?"

"Good plan. By then I should be finished painting and have the estimate on the glass rail for the pool."

"Fantastic. What about you, Kristi?"

"I'm shopping for storage baskets and boxes this morning, and then I'll be working at home. I need to finish the curtains." She had another project in mind for Nate's place and she needed to shop for supplies for that, too, but she wasn't ready to tell Sam and Claire about it. Not yet. Mostly because they were out of time, but also because it didn't exactly fit with her plan to take things slow.

Chapter Eleven

Kristi quickly cleared the junk mail, candle holders, dog leash and her morning teacup from the kitchen table, and then she set down the bag of supplies she'd brought home from the craft store. On the counter between the kitchen and eating area, she carefully spread the photo strips she had surreptitiously collected at Nate's place. He didn't seem to notice they were missing, and until she was finished with them, she was keeping her fingers crossed he wouldn't.

She picked up one of the most recent strips and turned it over. She was impressed that he had carefully noted the date, and sometimes the occasion, on the back of each strip. How many guys would think to do that? Not many. Certainly none she knew.

In Nate's case, these systematically labeled photo strips resembled the work he was doing in his gazebo-slash-greenhouse. She had watched him out there when he didn't know it. Every plant had an ID label attached to its pot, and all the data he gathered was entered into his computer and double-checked for accuracy.

He didn't apply the same level of detail to everything—the foyer closet attested to that—but he paid attention to the things that really mattered. She loved that about him. No, she *liked* that about him.

She set the photo back on the counter, faceup, and emptied the craft store bags. Four white shadow boxes. An assortment of scrapbooking paper, a package of miniature clothespins, a roll of twine. Plus the box of screws with little eyelets on the ends that she'd picked up at the hardware store.

She had never done anything like this for a client before, and she sincerely hoped she wasn't overstepping. It had taken a while for her to come up with a project to display the photographs without damaging them or altering them in any way. If he totally hated her idea, at least he could remove the strips and put them back on the fridge.

"Stop worrying about it." She loved to dream up DIY projects, and she was sure this one would be a winner.

She pulled the measuring tape out of her basket of sewing supplies and double-checked the widths of the shadow boxes and photo strips. Each box would easily hold six strips, with room to spare.

She planned to make two boxes for the girls' bedroom—one for each of them—and another for Nate's office. The fourth could go in the family room, or he might even want to have it in his office at the university. Did university professors do that sort of thing?

At the craft store she hadn't been able to decide on what to use for the backdrop in each box, so she'd purchased more paper than she needed. Now she spread the sheets on the table and studied them.

The polka-dot print in three shades of purple on white was an obvious choice for Martha. She was torn between two pink designs for Molly but finally settled on the peppermint-pink butterfly silhouettes, again on white. The two patterns complemented one another, fit the design scheme she'd created for their bedroom and still personalized each girl's keepsake.

For Nate's office she decided on a sheet with a mossy-green solid background and a plant motif in a slightly lighter shade. She compared it to the paint sample she'd chosen. Perfect.

She couldn't decide on a background for the fourth box, so she set it aside and turned to the photographs. Should she randomly choose six strips for each box? Unable to decide, she sorted them chronologically.

The first few were taken when the girls were about a year and a half old. Nate said he'd started taking them when his wife was in the hospital and too sick to visit with their young daughters. As toddlers, Molly and Martha were adorable with their wispy blond curls and innocent smiles. Martha was sucking her thumb in at least half of the shots.

Kristi's chest went tight. She had allowed these two little cuties to carve themselves a large niche in her life, and there would be a big hole in her heart when the house was finished and she and their father were no longer pretending they had a thing for each other. Ending the fake relationship would leave another hole. If she wasn't careful, her poor heart was going to resemble a piece of Swiss cheese.

"That has to be the dumbest analogy for a broken heart I've heard." Besides, her heart could only be broken if she let it.

She laughed at her own nonsense and woke Hercules from his slumbers on a sunny patch of the floor near the patio doors. He cocked a quizzical ear, then scratched at the glass. She slid the door open for him, checking to be sure the gate to the common area was securely latched so he couldn't get away.

Setting her emotions aside and letting her creative instincts take over, she skimmed the strips again and selected six, each containing at least one photograph of the girls kissing Nate's cheeks. She set those with the green paper she'd chosen for Nate's shadow box and looked for similar themes for each girl. For Molly, some of the sillier pictures, like the one with the girls making bunny ears over their dad's head. For Martha she chose several of the more serious poses, including one in which they were looking at a book with dinosaurs on the cover.

The front door opened. "Mom?"

"In here, sweetie."

Jenna came through the kitchen, grabbing a bottle of water from the fridge on her way.

"How was the water park?"

"Fun. It's hot out, though." She flopped onto a chair, unscrewed the bottle cap and took a long drink. "Ah, I needed that. On the way home, Abbie's mom took us to the drive-through for ice cream."

"That was nice of her."

Jenna took another drink and capped the bottle. "What are you working on?"

"Shadow boxes for Nate's place."

"Cool." She picked up a photo strip, put it down and picked up another. "Wow. They have a lot of these."

"I know. Aren't they adorable? I've been finding them all over the house, so I decided to figure out some way to display them."

"So you're putting them in these frames?"

"Yes, I thought this would be a fun way to display them. I'm going to screw these little eyelets into the inside of the boxes." She opened the package and took out two of them. "Like this."

She measured and marked the inside of each frame, then with a small pair of pliers from her craft box, inserted the screws.

"Now I'll run a piece of this twine from one ring to the

other to make a little clothesline. If you'd like to give me a hand, you could measure and cut four of those."

"Sure." Jenna dug a pair of scissors out of the sewing basket. "Oh, these are so cute!" She picked up the package of mini clothespins. "You're going to use these to hang the pictures on the clothesline? Neat idea."

"I thought so." She hoped Nate would agree.

While Jenna installed the twine clotheslines, Kristi glued the colored paper to the backboard for three of the boxes. Then together they hung the photo strips, attached the backing and stood back to admire their handiwork.

"What do you think?" Kristi asked.

"You always have such neat ideas. It'd be fun to make one of these for Abbie for her birthday."

"Good idea."

"And it's obvious you're totally into this guy."

"What?"

"You asked what I thought. I'm telling you." Jenna drained her water bottle, got up and nonchalantly tossed it in the recycling bin in the cupboard under the sink.

Smarty pants. "Nate and I hardly even know each other."

"You've been on three dates in less than a week."

"Three? How did you come up with that?"

"You went out Friday night. I babysat, remember? Then you went out on Saturday, and I babysat again."

"Saturday wasn't a date. We went to look at furniture."

"And then you went for lunch. That *totally* makes it a date."

Kristi let that slide.

"And there was Sunday brunch. Also a date."

Arguing would be pointless. The whole purpose of going together to these family events was so everyone would believe they *were* dating. She hated to deceive her daughter, but she hated the thought of having Bernie Halverson show up at Aunt Wanda and Uncle Ted's barbecue even more.

"Do you mind?" Kristi asked, steering the conversation in a different direction. "I know you were mad about the way Nate handled the whole makeup thing when you looked after the girls on Saturday."

"We talked," Jenna said. "He apologized, and now we have an understanding."

An understanding? "Um…what does that mean, exactly."

"He has to treat you well and not yell at you like he yelled at me."

Jenna's cat-that-got-the-cream smile had her feeling a teensy bit uncomfortable. "Is that what the two of you talked about in the kitchen?"

"Yep."

"And you said that to him?"

"Yep. I told him I'd be pis—" Jenna cut herself off. "I'd be *angry* if anyone does anything to hurt you."

Yesterday, after Nate and Jenna had talked in the kitchen at his parents' place, he had assured her everything was "better than okay." Nate had definitely looked more relaxed, even a little relieved, and she remembered thinking at the time how she would like to have been a fly on the wall for that conversation.

Kristi laughed and gave her daughter a hug. "Have I told you lately what a great kid you are?"

Jenna hugged her back. "Not lately."

"Well, I'm telling you now. You're a good kid, and I love you."

"I love you, too, Mom. And since I'm so great and you love me so much, maybe I should get a new cell phone. Abbie's getting an iPhone for her birthday."

"Nice try. You know we can't afford one."

"Yeah, well, it was worth a shot."

Hercules slipped in through the narrow opening in the patio door, skittered across the floor and yipped around Jenna's ankles.

"Hey, little buddy. Let's go upstairs. Can I use your laptop, Mom? I want to check email and Facebook."

"Sure. It's upstairs in my bedroom."

Alone again, Kristi took another long look at her handiwork. The three shadow boxes had been so easy to make, and she was sure Nate and the girls would love them. She was uncertain what to use for the background of the fourth box. It would depend on where Nate wanted to hang it. For either the family room or his office at the university, something more neutral would be best. That ruled out the other paper she'd purchased at the craft store. Unless…

She dug her camera out of her bag, took it out of the case and turned it on. She had taken some photographs at the birthday brunch yesterday, promising to email them to Britt as soon as she had a chance to download them. She scrolled through the photographs till she got to the one she'd taken of Nate, Molly and Martha. If she converted it to black-and-white, gave it a washed-out look and had a large enough print made to cover the backboard of the shadow box, it would be perfect.

"Brilliant, even if I do say so myself."

She would get it ready as soon as Jenna was off the computer. Instead of turning off the camera, though, she studied the photograph. Nate hadn't dressed up for the occasion, but he hadn't worn one of his science-geek T-shirts, either. He had attempted to style his hair—she could tell because it smelled so good—but a couple of wavy, finger-tempting strands fell over his forehead as though they had a mind of their own. As always, though, his eyes were what drew her to the photograph, to him. They were honest, intelligent and so, so blue. In this shot, he was looking at his daughters, not the camera, and the intensity of his love for them filled Kristi with longing. As a child she had ached for that kind of fatherly love, and since Jenna was born, she had ached for it on her behalf.

Molly and Martha were adorably cute in their party dresses, and while the loss of their mother at such a young age was heartbreakingly sad, there was no lack of love in their lives.

She clicked the camera off and hastily stuffed it back in her bag.

Get a grip. She'd met Nate less than a week ago, had broken every single one of her rules about setting a good example and not having a man in her life, and now—even though there was absolutely no logic to it—she was falling for this guy.

One thing was certain. Jenna did not need to worry about Nate hurting her mother. If Kristi ended up with a broken heart when this was all over and done with, she would only have herself to blame.

BY THE END of the week Nate had decided that if anyone ever needed anything done around the home, these were the women to call. More than once Kristi had insisted there should be fewer items in a room, and the things that were there should have more importance. Now, looking around, he could see she was right.

The week had flown by and today the house was a hub of activity, with Kristi putting the final touches on the family room and Sam outside, hammering and sawing and, at that precise moment, running a power tool of some kind. Jenna was here, too, keeping the girls entertained in their newly refurbished bedroom. He should be doing more to help, but after several years of managing on his own, his home was now overrun with women. There were feminine touches everywhere, and he liked it.

Kristi breezed in the front door with an armload of cushions and he stood there, breathing in her fragrance. He was used to it now, but every once in a while it sneaked up on him and set his senses on fire. He was going to miss that, too. A lot.

"Anything I can do to help?" he asked, not wanting her to disappear just yet.

She stopped. "There is. Two of these cushions, the blue ones, are for the guest room. Can you run them down there for me?"

"Sure." As he tugged on one, she lost her grip on the entire armload and down the pillows went in a jumble of color and patterned fabric. Together the two of them knelt to retrieve the wayward cushions, but they ended up reaching for the same one. Pulling on it brought them closer together, the cushion caught between them. Kristi was laughing, her eyes more gray than green in this light, and he felt himself free-falling.

The condom incident flashed into his mind, then it was overshadowed by the prospect of kissing her again. The possibility had occupied most of his waking thoughts for the past week, and every dream for as many nights. He just needed to figure out a way to make it happen.

She was within kissing distance right now. All he had to do was lean in a little.

She went quiet and her eyes darkened.

Kiss her.

He wanted to, badly, but the happy voices of children playing down the hall and the sounds of backyard construction drifted into his consciousness, reminding him this was not the right time. One kiss wouldn't be enough, not now and not ever.

He let go of the cushion, stood and offered her a hand up.

"Thanks."

"You're welcome."

"I'll be right back." He scooped up the two blue cushions and left her to gather up the others.

Kristi had spent the week working her way from room to room, and she had started by turning the spare room into a guest room after the girls' belongings and the contents of his office were returned to their rightful places. Not that he ever had overnight guests, but this was meant to show the new owners they could. Or they might fill these rooms with more children. Now that he'd settled things with Alice and the house was looking so good, he was starting to regret his decision to sell it.

Before Kristi arrived on the scene, the bed in the spare room had been buried beneath boxes of Christmas decorations and an assortment of winter coats, and a treadmill had taken up a considerable bit of floor space. Now the room was, in his sister's words, "a study in beige and white."

He didn't know what Kristi wanted to do with the pillows so he tossed them on the bed. On his way back to the family room, he stopped at Molly and Martha's room. They were sprawled on the floor with Jenna, Gemmy and Hercules, and surrounded by LEGO.

"How's it going?" he asked.

"Good." Jenna offered a green brick to Molly. "Is this the kind you're looking for?"

"Yup." Molly held up two bricks and snapped them together. "Daddy, we're building a town."

Martha, head bent, was intent on choosing pieces for her construction project.

He was glad Kristi had suggested Jenna watch the girls while he helped her get the house organized. Now that school was out, she wanted to keep her daughter busy so she didn't spend her summer vacation hanging out with boys at the mall. Jenna was great with the girls, and they adored her. Seeing the three blond heads huddled over their LEGO village, it struck him that anyone who saw them like this might think they were sisters. There was a crazy thought. If Molly and Martha had a big sister, that would make him the father of a teenager. Definitely a crazy thought.

He shifted his attention away from the girls and scanned their room. It had been finished earlier this week—Kristi had even sewn curtains for it—and Molly's and Martha's furniture had been moved back in. Sam's closet organizer worked like a charm, and so had Kristi's suggestion that they replace the mountain of stuffed animals with a few favorites and framed photos of the ones they weren't keeping. He never would have thought of that, and even if he had, he sure wouldn't have expected the girls to go along with it.

Kristi's curtains looked every bit as good as anything from a store. Probably better, but what did he know? They were plain white and the edges were trimmed with purple, pink and green ribbons sewn in horizontal and vertical stripes. The girls loved them, and his sister, Britt, claimed they were magazineworthy. He didn't know if home stagers normally sewed custom-made curtains for their clients, but he liked that this one did.

Molly and Martha had been reluctant to take down the tent in the family room, but Kristi convinced them to put it away, saying that when the new sofa was delivered, she needed their help arranging the furniture for optimal TV viewing. The tent had then been packed away with the same excitement as when they'd pitched it. Kristi was great with kids, and watching her with his girls was like taking a master class in parenting. And she'd managed to arrange the new sofa so it faced the TV and afforded a view of the patio.

Sam had spent most of the week working outside. She'd brought in a pool maintenance company to clean and fill the pool, treat the water and make sure the pump was in working order. True to her word, she had arranged to have a glass railing installed around the pool. It looked amazing, it was safe for children—his or those of a prospective buyer—and the glass virtually disappeared, leaving a clear sight line to the pool from anywhere in the yard. The place was starting to look more like a magazine spread than his home.

Yesterday he had collected the last set of data from his plants in the greenhouse. Then he had hauled the plants through the garage and out to the driveway, and Sam had been right behind him, stripping away the plastic off the pergola and sanding the wood in preparation for a fresh coat of stain.

The phone rang, and Alice's number appeared on call display. What now? He didn't want to answer it, but with so many people around he couldn't let it just ring until it went to voice mail. He sighed and took the call.

"Nate, how are things going with the house?"

"Good, thanks." He paused and waited for the other shoe to drop. When Alice called she never got right to the point.

"Is there much more to do?"

"I don't think so." He honestly didn't know, but Kristi definitely seemed to have things well in hand.

"We know you're busy so Fred and I decided we would help you out by taking the girls off your hands tomorrow night."

Instead of sounding like an offer, it was more of a demand.

"We'll pick them up around lunchtime and drop them off sometime Sunday morning before we go golfing."

He could decline their offer by making up some sort of excuse, but Molly and Martha did enjoy spending time with their grandparents. And having the girls gone for the evening would give him a chance to set something up with Kristi.

"That sounds good, Alice. I'll have the girls ready to go by noon."

"Oh." The surprise in Alice's voice implied that she had expected him to put up an argument. "All right, then. We'll be there at noon."

He set the phone back in its cradle and pondered the possibilities that had just opened up. He could offer to take Kristi out to dinner and a movie. No, that sounded too much like a traditional date, and despite what they wanted everyone else to believe, between them they were still taking the "we're not really dating" stand.

From the sliding doors in the family room, he surveyed the backyard, watching Kristi and Sam carefully position the patio furniture. Kristi stepped back, shook her head, and they moved a pair of lounge chairs closer to one corner of the pool.

"Much better," he heard her say. "This is a perfect spot for parents to sit and keep an eye on the children while they're swimming."

That's it, he thought. Dinner here, by the pool. He could barbecue something. Steak? No, better make it burgers. It would just be the two of them but he would keep it casual, make it sound as though it was his way of saying thank you for all the work she'd done.

Kristi had performed nothing short of a miracle. He hadn't realized that the cluttered and untidy house had been weighing him down, or that cleaning and decluttering would also sweep away some of the grief and much of the guilt that had been pressing in on him. She was walking around the pool, examining her handiwork from every angle, and he couldn't take his eyes off her.

She looked deceptively sporty in what he'd come to realize was her customary work attire. Trim black exercise pants cropped below the knee and low-cut white sport socks in a pair of canvas sneakers. Today's were red to match her pullover. Her hair was pulled back in a ponytail and held in place with a red-and-white scrunchie. No way did she look old enough to be the mother of a fourteen-year-old.

He slid the screen open and stepped out onto the patio. Kristi whirled around, smiled at him and tripped over an ottoman. Sam caught her and laughed, and Nate had a pretty good idea she was laughing at the two of them.

"I'll just run out to my truck to get the solar patio lights you want to use around the yard," she said. "If you need anything else moved, maybe Nate can give you a hand." She winked at him on her way to the house. "You don't mind, do you?"

He returned the wink. "Not at all. Happy to help." And more than happy to have a few minutes alone with Kristi. "What would you like me to do?"

"If you could set up the umbrella while I arrange the seat cushions, we'll be done."

Easy enough. He angled the umbrella pole through the centre of the table and anchored it in the base below.

"Would you like to come over for dinner tomorrow night?" He held his breath and waited.

She stopped what she was doing and stared at him for a full five seconds. "You mean like a family thing?"

"No. The girls will be at their grandparents'."

"So just the two of us. Like a…date."

She was avoiding emotional entanglements until her daughter was older, so this dating thing—real or not—was as new to her as it was to him. Best to take it slow. "No, not exactly. I was just thinking it seems a shame to have everything looking so good and not use it. So I thought, with the girls gone, we could throw some burgers on the barbecue, nothing fancy."

"That sounds nice." She arranged the last seat cushion and then looked up at him again. "Jenna has a sleepover tomorrow night. It's her friend Abbie's birthday."

Sleepovers were good. Molly and Martha were having one, Jenna was having one. That meant he and Kristi could spend all evening together. And sleepover suddenly took on a whole new meaning.

"Well, good," he said. "It'll just be the two of us."

"And the dogs. You don't mind if I bring Hercules?"

"Not at all."

"Okay, then. It's a…" She didn't finish the sentence, but they both knew what she had almost said. "What time?"

"How does seven sound?"

"Seven sounds great. I'll be here. And since you're making dinner, I'll bring dessert."

He liked the sound of that.

Sam returned with an armload of boxes and a sly smile. "I hope I'm not interrupting anything."

"Not at all." Nate had accomplished everything he'd set out to do.

Chapter Twelve

By six o'clock on Saturday, Kristi had tried on half the things in her closet and still hadn't found anything to wear. Jeans and a T-shirt looked too casual. It was a warm evening so she could get away with shorts, but they would show too much leg. A skirt and top made her feel as though she was attending a business meeting. Her eye kept straying to the vintage-inspired boat-necked dress hanging on the inside of her closet door. She'd made it to wear to her ten-year high school reunion a couple of years ago. It was a nice subdued shade of pale yellow, knee-length with a full skirt. It was a bit dressy, but was it too dressy? Not if she wore her white cashmere cardigan over it, she decided. She held up the jeans again and studied herself in the mirror.

"Mom, you can't wear jeans," Jenna said from the doorway.

"What's wrong with jeans?"

"Nothing. They're just not you. You wear jeans to do housework or take Hercules for a walk, but you'd never wear them on a date."

True. She loved pretty clothes and bright colors. That she would even consider blue jeans simply showed how desperate she was to convince herself this was not a date.

Oh, it was a date, all right. Her legs were shaved and everything.

"Wear the dress," Jenna said. "It looks great on you."

Kristi fingered the soft fabric. Her daughter was right. It was a very pretty dress, totally feminine, and she did look good in it. With a white belt instead of the silver one she'd worn to the reunion, flats instead of heels… Okay, she was definitely wearing the dress.

"What time is Abbie's mom picking you up?"

"They'll be here in a few minutes."

"And her parents are supervising the entire evening?"

"Mom! We've gone over this a hundred times."

Kristi made a face at the mirror. This was the second time they'd talked about this, maybe the third. Definitely not the hundredth. She still hadn't found the right time for her and Jenna to have "the talk," though, and there were going to be boys at this party. Only till ten o'clock, and then it would just be Abbie, Jenna and another girl for the sleepover. Still, a lot could happen between six-thirty and ten.

The doorbell rang.

"There they are. See you tomorrow, Mom."

Kristi reached for Jenna to give her a hug, but she was gone. "I'll see you tomorrow morning," she called down the stairs.

"Okay, see ya!" And that was all the goodbye she got before the front door slammed.

Jenna will be fine, she told herself. *It's you I'm worried about.* Not that anything would happen between her and Nate tonight. They were both too cautious and level-headed for that.

She shrugged out of the housecoat she'd put on after her shower, slipped the dress off its hanger and held it up for one last look. Nate would like it, she was sure of that, but she hoped that by dressing up for a casual dinner of burgers by the pool, she wasn't sending the wrong message. Or maybe dressing up was the right message.

AT FIVE MINUTES to seven, Nate warned himself against checking the clock every thirty seconds and keeping track of how many minutes ticked by until Kristi arrived. They'd have the whole evening together. Just the two of them, no kids to offer up a distraction, no extended family keeping tabs on them. He could still hardly believe his luck.

He had given her a key so she could come and go as she needed, but tonight she rang the bell. She was right on time, and she took his breath away. He would have waited a lifetime for this woman. Hell, he already had.

"Come in." He reached for Hercules's travel bag and set it on the floor. The dog started yipping right away, and a drooling Gemmy loped into the foyer to greet him. He opened the Yorkie's bag, and he skittered out, touching noses with the Saint.

"Looks like they have a date, too," he said.

Kristi laughed, and for once he wished he could take his lead from the dogs, shove propriety aside and kiss her. Right here, right now. Of course being a dog and acting like a dog were two different things, and tonight he was determined to do this right.

"You look amazing."

"Thank you. I was leaning toward jeans, but my daughter said I should wear the dress."

He wondered if it would be appropriate to thank Jenna the next time he saw her. Not likely. "I'm glad she did. Come in."

"Thanks."

They were both feeling awkward and overly formal, and he would be glad when they were sitting by the pool with a glass of wine.

Kristi was carrying a small box, and that's when he remembered the dessert.

"Would you like me to take that?" he asked.

"No, thanks. It's sort of a surprise, and I don't want to ruin the fun."

"Bring it into the kitchen, then."

They walked through the house together, and when they got to the kitchen, Kristi opened the fridge and tucked the container inside. "Whipped cream," she said. "It needs to stay chilled."

It's just dessert, he reminded himself, but the words *whipped cream* had his heart and his mind racing ahead to later in the evening.

Down, boy. It's just dessert.

"Let's go sit outside," he said. He slid the screen open and the dogs dashed out ahead of them.

Kristi followed and stopped just outside the door.

"Is everything okay?"

"Yes," she said. "More than okay. It's really beautiful out here." She laughed at her own words. "I'm really pleased with the way it turned out."

"So am I. You've done an amazing job." He couldn't remember ever meeting anyone like her. His entire adult life had revolved around the university. The women he met were smart, serious, studious. Heather included. Kristi was every bit as smart and creative, but with more joie de vivre.

She touched his arm, lightly, and the effect was electric. "I remember the first day I was here, thinking how unfortunate it was that you had this amazing outdoor space but it wasn't being used. Have you and the girls had a chance to get in the pool yet?"

"We had a swim yesterday afternoon before supper. They were so excited…I can't even tell you."

"I'm glad."

"Come on. Let's sit. Would you like something to drink? There's white wine in the ice bucket. I remember that's what you had at Britt's birthday party. I also have beer. A dark ale." He held up the bottle. "And a lager that's a little less...dark. And I'll stop talking now."

"The white wine sounds great," she said. "I'm not much of a beer drinker."

Good to know. He opened the bottle with as much flourish as he could muster while Kristi settled into one of the four club chairs she and Sam had arranged in the pergola. He handed a glass to her and took the chair next to her, grateful that the close proximity still afforded a view of her legs stretched in front of her and demurely crossed at the ankles. He could get used to this.

"So..." She smiled at him and he almost forgot what he wanted to say. "Ah, Jenna's at a sleepover tonight?"

"Yes, her friend Abbie is turning fourteen so it's a birthday-party-slash-sleepover. I had some misgivings about it."

"Why is that?" He was genuinely interested, since someday he, too, would be navigating life with teenage girls.

"There'll be boys at the party. Just till ten o'clock, not for the sleepover, obviously."

He laughed. "A disappointing fact of life for them, I'm sure."

Kristi laughed, too, but there was little humor in it. "Tell me about it. Anyway, I spoke with Abbie's mom and she's assured me the party will be fully supervised, as will the sleepover after the boys leave."

"So no sneaking out to meet them once the parents have gone to bed."

"That's what we're counting on."

He debated whether or not to ask if they'd had "the talk." No, that would be way too personal.

"You're probably wondering if I talked to her about…"

"How did it go?" he asked.

"It didn't." She looked a little deflated. "I don't know why this is so difficult. We have a good relationship—we talk about all sorts of things, but this is really awkward. I'm afraid Jenna's going to think I'm lame and not take me seriously."

He could well imagine a safe sex demonstration involving a banana would seem lame to a teenager.

"You'd think there would be books on how to do this sort of thing," he said.

"Books?"

"Yes, books. Books for parents, books for teenagers."

"I'm not sure about parenting by the book. They can be helpful but I think it's up to parents to decide what they need to tell their kids, and when their kids are ready to hear it."

"Good point." He hoped he remembered that when his time came to make these decisions.

"And I'm not sure how effective a safe sex handbook for teens would be anyway." Her smile curved in a way that could only be described as mischievous. "Most kids wouldn't bother to read it. They'd just look at the pictures."

He laughed. "Girls, too? I'd have thought…hoped?… that maybe just boys did things like that."

"I wish." But she was laughing, too.

He set his beer on the table and stood up. "More wine?"

"Not just yet, thanks. Maybe with dinner."

Dinner. Right. "I'll start the barbecue."

"Were Molly and Martha excited about spending the night with their grandparents?"

"They seemed to be. I just hope they don't come home with more stuff. Alice likes to take them shopping."

"How has she been since you told her the girls weren't going to be in the pageant?"

He shrugged. "She hasn't said a word about it."

"Nothing?"

"Not one word. It's almost too easy, and I'm not sure if that's a good thing or a bad thing."

Kristi looked thoughtful. "I think you should just relax. This is what you wanted, right?"

She was probably right. If he was honest with himself, it had been a long time since he really thought about what he wanted.

"It's just that she has a mind of her own, and once she's made it up, there's usually no changing it." He didn't know why he was telling her this, except that she was easy to talk to, and he liked her levelheaded, no-nonsense approach.

"It can be hard to set boundaries with family. Was it like that when your wife was alive?"

Heather and her mother had been very different people. "Heather always made it seem as though she was going along with her mother, then she usually did whatever she wanted to do."

Even as he said it, he could see the flaw in that approach. He'd bet Kristi saw it, too.

"I can relate," she said. "It seems like an easy way to avoid conflict, and for a while it works, but eventually whatever it is you're trying to avoid will sneak up and bite you on the butt."

No kidding. Like Alice's crazy scheme to enter the girls in some kind of beauty pageant.

"How do you like your burgers?" he asked.

"Well done, and I mean really well done. Black on the outside and absolutely no pink on the inside."

More info to file away. He slid a patty onto the grill for her. He'd give it a couple of minutes before he started his.

"I usually have a head-on approach to setting boundaries," Kristi said. "Trust me, when Molly and Martha are teenagers, you'll get lots of practice. I've been putting off this talk with Jenna, but now that you and I have had this conversation, I know I can't keep doing that. She's a good kid, and I trust her, but it's time. As she gets older and becomes more independent, I want her to have all the information she needs to make the right choices."

"When Molly and Martha get to that age, I'll call you for advice."

For the life of him, he couldn't decipher the look she gave him. Probably wondering, like he was, if they would still be friends ten years from now. Ha. Even now he didn't want to be just friends. Taking their relationship to the next level would definitely rule out the possibility of them still being "friends" a decade from now.

"What I meant—"

"I think I know what you mean. I hope you do call."

"Oh, that's good." That was very good. He tossed his burger onto the barbecue next to hers.

She took a sip of her wine. "Here we are, spending a nice evening together, and we're talking about our kids and our families. Why don't you tell me something about yourself?"

He was all for it. "What would you like to know?"

"What you teach at the university, your research, how you got interested in studying plants."

"How much time do you have?" He was only half joking.

While he prepared their burgers and served the salad he'd made to go with it, he gave her the *Reader's Digest* version of his life as a graduate student and touched on the research he'd done for his PhD thesis while hoping he didn't sound too boring.

"What about you?" he asked when she joined him at the patio table. "When did you decide you wanted to be an interior decorator?"

"I'm not sure. I always knew I wanted to do something creative, and when I finally went to college after my divorce, I was seriously considering graphic arts."

While they ate, she told him how she had put herself through a two-year diploma program at community college while juggling single-parenthood, how she'd met Sam and Claire, and how they'd made the decision to open Ready Set Sold. He was already impressed by her, and now his admiration reached a whole new height.

"That was the best burger I've ever had. Are you ready for dessert?" she asked when he pushed his plate away.

"I can't wait to find out what's in that box." And what else was in store for them tonight.

She smiled coyly. "Why don't you sit here while I clear the plates and serve?"

"Sounds like a plan." He watched her walk toward the house, then refilled their wineglasses. She might not want any more, given that she had to drive home. Unless things went the way he hoped and her car spent the night in his driveway.

Kristi returned carrying a pair of bowls with both dogs following closely. "I thought they might like to have their dinner out here." She set the dogs' dishes on the patio. "Be right back."

This time she came back with two cupcakes on a single plate. Cupcakes? That was the surprise? Not that there was anything wrong with her cupcakes—they were delicious—but she had implied something a little less kid's birthday party and a little more grown-up. And then he saw them close up, a pair of chocolate cupcakes in red foil cups, generously topped with a swirl of whipped cream and a red maraschino cherry, stem and all.

Kristi slid her chair closer to his and sat down, wrapping him again in the fragrance he'd now come to associate with her.

"What are you wearing?" he asked. "That fragrance?"

"French lilac. Do you like it?"

"I do."

"Good answer."

He put her wineglass in her hand, picked up his, touched his to hers. Then, from the top of one cupcake he plucked a cherry by its stem, but instead of eating it himself, he offered it to her.

Their gazes met and connected. She opened her mouth and accepted it, closing her teeth around the sweet fleshy fruit as he gently tugged the stem away.

"Mmmm," she murmured, chewing it slowly, washing it down with another sip of wine. Then she licked her lips, and he was a goner.

He kissed her, losing himself in the taste of the wine and her, and she kissed him back with a hunger that had nothing to do with dessert. He had planned to invite her to swim with him, hoping she would accept, hoping even more that she hadn't brought a swimsuit with her. Now he had only one thing on his mind.

He pulled back a little, reconnected with her deep green gaze and gradually became aware of hundreds of tiny white lights twinkling in the backyard shrubbery. It was magical.

Kristi was smiling. "Pretty, isn't it? Sam put the lights on a timer."

It was magical. So was she. "Stay the night?" he asked.

The answer he needed to hear came in the form of a kiss, and he was happier than he had been in a very long time.

Chapter Thirteen

Kristi woke to the sound of running water. As she rolled onto her back and stretched, she drowsily thought how unusual it was for Jenna to be the first one up. Wait a minute...

Her eyes snapped open and she stared at the ceiling. Nate's ceiling. Nate's *bedroom* ceiling. She was alone in the bed and the shower was running in the en suite.

She held up the covers, took a quick look underneath and hastily pulled them down again. She was naked.

"Of course you're naked." Now wide-awake, she had a vivid recollection of Nate undressing her last night, of her returning the favor, of tumbling in his bed together.

How much had she had to drink? Two glasses of wine? Three? No, she was sure it was only two. Not enough to blame her impulsive behavior on being tipsy. And now she was in his bed without a stitch on and he could appear any minute and they'd be naked together, in broad daylight.

No way. She flung the sheet away, leaped out of bed and grabbed her clothes. She'd slept with a man she'd met a week and a half ago, and on their first real date.

Way to set an example, Mom.

What had she been thinking? And where was her underwear?

Screw it. Braless, she wriggled into her dress and

zipped it up. On the other side of the bed she found her panties and pulled them on. From the back of a chair across the room, one bra strap peeked from beneath the shirt Nate had been wearing last night. She snagged the undergarment and ran, barefoot and silent, down the hall.

In the family room she found her shoes where she'd kicked them off as she and Nate had stumbled in from the patio, with only one thing and one destination in mind. Her handbag was on the kitchen counter where she'd left it. She grabbed it and stuffed her bra inside.

She was halfway to the front door when she remembered Hercules. *Where's your head?* His travel bag was in the family room and so was he, curled up next to Gemmy's head, sound asleep.

"Come on, boy," she whispered. Ignoring his whimpers, she whisked him into the bag and zipped it shut. "Sorry, Herc. We have to get out of here."

From the foyer she listened for sounds coming from down the hallway. Relieved to hear the shower still running, she slipped out the front door. She hated herself for taking the coward's way out, but she couldn't face him. Not this morning, maybe not ever. She was not the kind of woman who slept with a guy on the first date. Correction, she didn't used to be.

NATE CRANKED OFF the shower. He hadn't had the heart to disturb Kristi, she'd been sleeping so soundly, but as he dried himself off he contemplated how he would wake her after he slid back under the covers. There were a lot of options, and he liked every single one of them.

Or maybe she'd be awake by now, waiting for him. He fastened the towel around his waist but stopped in the doorway, taking in the rumpled sheets and empty bed. No sign of her clothes, either. Hmm. She must have gone into the kitchen, maybe to make coffee. Without bothering to swap the towel for his robe, he went to find her.

Several minutes later, reality slowly sank in. Kristi was gone. While he was in the shower, she'd taken her dog and snuck out. A quick check outside confirmed that her van was gone, too.

What the hell?

Last night had been amazing. At least, for him it had. It had been their first real date, and thanks to the previous fake ones, there had been none of those awkward first-date moments. Their conversation felt natural, comfortable, and by the time they got to dessert they were both ready to take things to the next level. He was damn sure of that. They couldn't get out of their clothes and into bed fast enough. This morning apparently the reverse had also been true, for her at least.

What the hell? he thought again.

Sure, he was a little out of practice, but sex was one of those things you never forgot. Like riding a bicycle. There was solid scientific evidence to prove how those memories were stored in various parts of the brain, and how the brain retrieved them.

"Seriously? You've just been dumped in the worst possible way by the hottest, sexiest woman you've ever met, and all you can think about is some stupid scientific theory?"

And it wasn't an everyday, garden-variety dumping. He'd been dumped by the woman he was in love with, dammit.

He prided himself on being a practical man. A week ago, he'd have said love at first sight only happened in the movies, not real life, but the truth was he'd fallen for her that first day. She'd breezed through his front door, tripping on his kids' boots and spilling his dog's water bowl, and blazed a trail straight into his heart.

Straight into his heart. "Geez, when did you turn into a poet?"

Since last night, maybe. And now that the shock…and, let's face it, the hurt…of her unexplained departure had sunk in, he was damn sure that his performance in bed wasn't the reason she'd bolted this morning. No way she'd faked those orgasms, he thought smugly. Not a chance. Last night had been every bit as good for her as it had for him. He and Kristi were compatible in and out of bed, so it had to be something else.

Maybe Jenna was in some kind of trouble and she'd had to rush off to help her. No, that didn't make sense. She would have said something before she left.

As he filled the coffeepot with water and scooped grounds into the basket, he systematically reviewed the conversations they'd had since she'd started the transformation on his house.

She resented her family's matchmaking attempts as much as he did his, and together they'd found a solution to put a stop to it.

Her ex was a deadbeat, but they'd established that Nate wasn't.

She was anxious about having "the talk" with Jenna because she didn't want her daughter to make the same mistakes she had.

None of those unexplained her unexpected departure.

Then he remembered something Jenna had said, that she saw stuff and heard stuff, and had figured out that her mother avoided relationships because she wanted to set a good example for her daughter.

Was that it? It was okay to have dinner with him, but

spending the night would send the wrong message? Jenna would never know she'd stayed if Kristi didn't tell her.

He grabbed a mug from the cupboard and set it on the counter, waiting for the machine to beep, and picked up the phone. There was only one way to find out. Ask her.

After five rings, her cheerful, upbeat greeting told him she was busy, apologized for not being able to take his call and invited him to leave a message.

"Kristi, it's Nate. Can we talk? Call me, okay?" He forced himself to hang up before he started to ramble.

"Busy my ass."

He poured coffee into his mug and carried it into the family room. Gemmy heaved herself up from her bed and ambled across the room to greet him. He opened the patio door for her.

"Go on. I'll take you for a walk after I get dressed." If Kristi had still been sleeping when he got out of the shower, he would have walked both dogs. Her little Yorkie and his huge Saint Bernard made an odd-looking couple, and their mutual infatuation was a humorous reminder that opposites attract.

Not unlike he and Kristi—the boring academic and the beautiful, spontaneous interior decorator. And yet there was common ground, including single-parenthood and challenges with their extended families. Jenna seemed fond of the twins, Molly and Martha adored her, the dogs were smitten with each other. He'd be the first to admit that he didn't always pick up on these things, but even he could see they were good together. Why couldn't she?

Maybe he should try calling her again.

"Yeah, right. Because your number showing up repeatedly on her phone isn't going to look desperate." And definitely more loser than deadbeat.

He needed a better plan, but first he needed to get

dressed and take Gemmy for a walk. That would give him a chance to think this through and figure out a way to convince Kristi that taking a chance on him was the right thing to do.

On the way to his bedroom, he stopped and looked into his office. Since she'd worked her magic in there, it was his favorite room in the house, and for as long as he lived here it would be a productive place to work. She had taken it from chaos to calm, and the room was organized and comfortable. It was as if she knew him better than he knew himself.

Five minutes later, as Nate was standing in the foyer, clipping the leash to Gemmy's collar, the doorbell rang. Kristi? Oh, yes. Please let it be her. He flung the door open and felt his smile fade. It was his mother-in-law, dropping off the girls an hour early.

"Alice, I wasn't expecting you. I was just going to walk the dog."

"Daddy!"

"Good morning, girls." He knelt and drew them in for a hug. "I missed you. Did you have fun?"

"Yup. Now we're going to build LEGO."

Molly pulled away, but Martha stayed close, with her head against his shoulder and her thumb in her mouth.

"Are you going to play with LEGO, too?" he asked.

She nodded and let her sister take her by the hand. He watched them disappear down the hall, each dragging a Hello Kitty backpack behind her. Then he stood and faced the woman at the door, who had yet to say a word, or even crack a smile. "Would you like to come in?"

She stepped in and closed the door, giving Gemmy a wide berth, not out of fear but because she simply didn't like dogs. She was carrying two clear plastic garment bags and the contents appeared to be dresses—one pale yellow, the other light purple. Dresses that Molly and Martha would have no occasion to wear, unless…

He didn't like the direction that thought was taking.

"Thanks for having the girls. Sounds like they had a good time."

Alice thrust the garment bags at him. "These are the girls' pageant dresses. They needed something for the evening-wear portion and I knew they wouldn't have anything suitable, so I took them shopping."

Nate stuck his hands in his pockets and stood his ground. He was having one of the crappiest mornings on record, and now this. "We've already discussed this, Alice. My daughters will not be entering a beauty pageant."

Her steely gaze didn't waiver. "You seem to forget that they're my granddaughters, and with Heather gone, they're all I have."

His temper was about to boil over when he remembered what Kristi said after he apologized for losing it over the girls playing with makeup.

Don't let this be about the pageant. Make it about your family—you and your daughters. She needs to know that you're open to her suggestions, but that in the end, you're the one who makes the decisions about what's best for them.

Kristi was right. He needed to put his foot down, once and for all, and he needed to do it now.

"Alice, you and Fred are an important part of the girls' lives, but you are not their parents. I am. I'm open to suggestions but I make the decisions, and I've decided there will be no pageant."

"But the girls want to do this, especially Molly. And Martha needs to get over her shyness—"

He hated to be rude, but this woman needed to learn how to take no for an answer. "I've already said no but you didn't seem to hear it, so let me say it again. *No.* The girls will not be in a pageant. And in the future, you will not discuss these things with my daughters until you've talked to me first."

He was on a roll now, and there was no stopping. "Molly'd never heard of these beauty pageants until you told her about them. And Martha's shyness is not a flaw, it's who she is. If you could accept that, then maybe you wouldn't feel the need to turn her into someone she's not." He stopped before he said *like you tried to do with your daughter.*

For the first time in all the years he'd known Alice, she was speechless. She opened and closed her mouth a couple of times before she managed to sputter, "Well, I never..."

No doubt that was true. She'd never heard these things, because no one had ever had the balls to say them. If not for Kristi, he might never have, either.

Gemmy, leash still attached to her collar, nudged the garment bags with her nose.

"For heaven's sake, get your dog under control," Alice said, jumping back a step and staring with disgust at the dog drool on her shoe.

Well placed, Gemmy. Nate tugged on the leash, lowering his head to pat the dog's back so Alice couldn't see his smile. "Sorry about that."

Without another word, Alice swung around and huffed out the door. She was furious, Nate got that, but she would come around. In the past, he would have felt like an ungrateful jerk but for the first time in what felt like forever, he was in control. Even Kristi's departure felt less about him, probably because it wasn't. He hoped she would have a change of heart but if she didn't, he would find a way to change it for her.

INSTEAD OF CRAWLING into bed and having a good cry when she got home from Nate's—and she'd been so tempted—Kristi forced herself to keep busy. After a quick shower, she pulled on a T-shirt and pair of yoga pants, went into the kitchen and hauled out her baking supplies.

A long time ago, she had figured out what she needed to do to ensure that her life didn't become a blueprint for Jenna's. She'd made the right decision, she was convinced of that. Last night she'd had a lapse in judgment, had let her feelings and Nate's hotness get the better of her, but she wasn't going down that road. Not now. The timing just wasn't right.

She was taking the second batch of cupcakes out of the oven when Jenna arrived home from her sleepover.

"Mom? I'm home." The front door slammed and a moment later Jenna appeared in the kitchen. "Wow, that's a lot of cupcakes. Is something wrong?"

"Of course not. Why?"

"'Cause when you're upset, you bake."

Jenna knew her too well. "I'm not upset," she said, hoping she sounded more convincing than she felt. "I'm going to put these in the freezer so they're ready for Aunt Wanda's barbecue."

Jenna leaned on elbows on the counter and studied her from the opposite side of the peninsula. "How was your date?"

Kristi avoided eye contact as she carefully removed the cupcakes from the pan and set them on a rack to cool. "It was fine."

"Did you and Nate have a fight?"

"No, of course not." Time to change the subject. "How was the party?"

"Awesome. Abbie's so lucky, her parents gave her an iPhone." She paused for effect, then continued, "After everybody left, we spent ages figuring out how it works and getting a bunch of apps set up and texting our friends."

"That's nice." Kristi turned off the oven and started to wash her baking dishes, fully expecting yet another explanation of how badly Jenna needed a new phone.

"Are you sure you're okay?" her daughter asked instead.

"I'm fine, sweetie. What are your plans for the rest of the day?"

Jenna yawned. "I'm going back to bed. We stayed up super late, and Abbie's mom made French toast for breakfast so we had to get up early."

Ordinarily Kristi would insist she stay awake and go to bed early tonight, but if Jenna went back to bed now, she would stop asking questions.

"I told Abbie she could come with us to Nate's tomorrow. Now that the pool's done, we can go for a swim."

Kristi snapped. "Jenna, you can't just invite people over there."

"But Nate said—"

"No *buts*. You should have asked *me* and I would have told you it's not appropriate for you to invite your friends to my client's home."

"Geez, you don't have to bite my head off. And since when is Nate a client? You guys are dating."

Calm down. It isn't fair to take this out on Jenna. "We're not dating. We've had a couple of casual…things. That's all. And I won't be working there tomorrow anyway."

"Why not?"

"I'm starting another project in the morning. Sam will finish up at Nate's." Which wasn't completely true. Or even remotely true. She didn't have another job lined up, and she had yet to talk to Sam about finishing this one. The part about her not working there was true, though. No way could she face him. Besides, a clean break was always best. Like tearing off a Band-Aid. It might hurt like hell at first, but not as much as prolonging the agony.

Jenna wasn't buying any of it. "You and Nate did have a fight."

Kristi turned back to the sink. "No, we didn't." They hadn't known each other long enough to fight.

Her phone buzzed and Jenna grabbed it off the counter.

"Don't answer that!"

"It's Nate," Jenna said.

Of course it was. He'd already left one message, now he most likely wanted to know why she hadn't called back. She reached for the phone and Jenna put it in her hand.

Kristi turned it off and tossed it aside.

"Why didn't you answer it?"

"I'm busy. I'll call him later."

"Right. 'Cause you're not upset, and you guys didn't have a fight, and you're just busy." Jenna rolled her eyes. "Whatever. I'm going to my room. Come on, Herc." She scooped the dog out of his basket and disappeared upstairs.

Once Kristi heard footsteps overhead, she quickly picked up her phone and checked her voice messages.

"Kristi, it's Nate. Again. Sorry to bother you. I want to make sure you're okay, and I want to tell you I had another talk with Alice. And this time she finally got the message."

"Daddy, I can't find my skipping rope."

"I'm on the phone, Molly. I'll help you look for it in a minute. Kristi? Hi, sorry about that. Anyway, give me a call when you get a chance. We should talk."

Kristi saved the message, then absently counted the rows of cupcakes cooking on the rack before they were blurred by tears. Then she opened a drawer, dropped her phone inside and closed it. Whatever she did, she would not call and tell him the skipping rope was in the toy box in the playhouse.

Chapter Fourteen

Kristi dragged herself out of bed on Monday morning, feeling like hell. Looking like it, too, she confirmed as she stood in front of the bathroom mirror, brushing her teeth. She pulled a robe over the T-shirt and boxers she'd worn to bed and went downstairs. Hercules scampered out of Jenna's room and followed, barking excitedly until she shooed him onto the patio.

She filled the kettle and put it on to boil, then checked her phone for messages. There weren't any. After two attempts to reach her, Nate had apparently given up.

"Can you blame him?"

She was tempted to replay the two he'd left yesterday, just to hear the sound of his voice, but she knew better. Instead she perused the assortment of teas in her cupboard and decided on a nice soothing cup of chamomile.

She was sitting with her fingers curled around the cup, staring at the four shadow boxes she'd made for Nate, when Jenna straggled down the stairs.

"Morning, Mom." She opened the fridge, poured herself a glass of orange juice and brought it to the table. "What are you doing?"

"Nothing."

"Are you still moping from yesterday?"

"I wasn't moping yesterday."

"Yes, you were, and you never do 'nothing.' You're always baking or sewing or working on some project on your laptop."

Kristi sipped her tea, which wasn't nearly calming enough. "I'm taking a day off."

"You said you were starting a new job today."

"I changed my mind."

Jenna sat across the table, gulped half the glass of juice before setting it in front of her, and leaned on her elbows. "Okay, spill. You've been grumpy as an old bear ever since you had dinner with Nate. What happened?"

"Nothing 'happened.' We just decided…I decided… that it's not going to work out."

"That's a bunch of crap."

A challenge sparkled in Jenna's eyes, but Kristi was too exhausted to take the bait.

"You like him, right? And he's totally crazy about you, so what's the problem?"

Kristi sighed. The role reversal caught her by surprise, but that didn't mean she owed her daughter an explanation. She was doing this for her, after all, but she was too young to understand why.

"It's not that simple."

"Seriously, Mom? You think I don't know what's going on here? It's like I said to Nate—"

Jenna talked to Nate? About this? And he didn't say anything? "When did you talk to him?"

"At the brunch thing when we were putting away the salads."

That's when he'd apologized for overreacting about putting makeup on Molly and Martha. She had no idea they'd talked about anything else. "What did you say to him?"

Jenna drained her juice glass. "I told him you hardly

ever go on dates because you think that if you do, you'll be setting a bad example for me."

"Where did you get that idea? And why would you say that to Nate?"

Jenna grinned. "Mom, I'm fourteen. I'm not a little kid. I hear you talking to Grandma and Aunt Wanda when they try to set you up with blind dates."

Kristi wondered what else her daughter knew, and decided there were some things she'd be better off not knowing.

"I turn down most of those dates because I'm just not interested...."

Her daughter laughed and shook her head. "I also know you're worried that I'll end up pregnant like you did, being a single mom like you were."

This was all bordering on too much information, especially this morning. Lack of sleep was making her head hurt and her eyes itch. She was in no mood for a teenage pep talk.

"I'm not a bad kid, Mom." She got up and put her glass in the dishwasher. "I know all about sex and where babies come from...and how not to make one."

And now Kristi's head was ready to explode. "I've been meaning to talk to you—"

"I know." Jenna was actually smirking now. "And I already know about this stuff, everybody does, and I'm not going to let it happen to me. I'm a good kid, I get good grades and just 'cause me and Abbie are hanging out with Matt and Jordan doesn't mean we're going to have sex with them. We're not ready for that."

Kristi got up and hugged her. Some of the all-aloneness she'd been feeling was replaced with a little relief and a whole lot of pride. Her daughter was a good kid, and maybe she worried more than she needed to.

"So, you know what this means, right?" Jenna asked.

With the sleeve of her bathrobe, Kristi dabbed the moisture from the corners of her eyes. "What does this mean?"

Jenna picked up the phone and handed it to her. "You can answer all those messages he left. I'll even go up to my room, give you some privacy."

Was Jenna right? Was it time she gave someone a chance? Tore down that fortress Sam had talked about? Maybe she should call him. Her heart thumped in her chest and her mouth went dry, and then the shadow boxes lined up on the sideboard caught her eye. Forget the phone. She had a better idea.

AFTER A LOUSY night of tossing and turning, Nate was in no mood to cope with anything, especially not two rambunctious girls clamoring to go swimming, to read a book about hippopotamuses, to put the tent back in the family room. He rarely asked for favors but while he waited for the coffeepot to do its thing, he called his mother and asked her to take the girls, using his work at the university and the final work on the house as an excuse.

He still didn't know what would happen this morning and that had him on edge. Would Kristi show up as though nothing had happened? Send someone else to wrap up the last things that needed to be done? He sure wasn't going to try calling again. If she needed time, he'd give her time. Even if it killed him.

From the kitchen, he walked through the dining room and into the living room. Except for the major pieces of furniture, these two rooms had been stripped bare and given a thorough floor-to-ceiling cleaning. Today they were to be staged. Kristi said they were her favorite rooms. When he and Heather bought the house, these had been his favorite rooms, too. And for some reason he had closed the doors and all but forgotten about them, as he'd done with other parts of his life. And then Kristi had come along and quite literally thrown the doors open.

Through the living room window, he watched Sam's truck pull up and park in front of the house. She didn't get out, though. She was on her cell phone, so he stood and watched and waited.

His patience was rewarded. Kristi's van pulled up behind Sam. In case they could see him from the street, and not wanting to be caught spying on them, he hustled back into the kitchen. Gemmy was sprawled on the family room carpet but the sound of the doorbell would have her up and running, so he opened the patio door and coaxed her outside.

The minutes ticked by. What were they doing out there? As he debated going to investigate, the bell rang. He rushed to the door, couldn't help himself, but he opened it slowly and did a terrible job of feigning surprise.

Kristi stood alone with the purple cupcake-printed purse slung over one shoulder and a big blue shopping bag in the other hand. After worrying this moment would never come, he wanted to pull her into his arms and not let her go for a very long time.

Play it cool, he told himself. "Hi."

"Hi."

"You didn't answer my calls. I thought you might not come."

"I almost didn't."

"Is Sam coming in?"

"Ah, no. She forgot to pick to the…widgets she needs to fix the…thingamajig." She couldn't keep a straight face and he laughed with her, grateful she'd found a way to break the ice and get rid of Sam so they could be alone.

"I asked her to give us a few minutes."

Good call. "Come in."

She stepped into the foyer and closed the door. "Where are the girls?"

"Spending the day with my mother."

"Good, because we should talk."

"Let's go in and sit down."

She set both bags on the family room floor and sat on the sofa. He joined her, thinking the last time they sat on it together was that day in the furniture store. She didn't say anything, and the only way he knew to start this conversation was to take the direct approach.

"Why did you leave yesterday? I was worried about you."

She folded her hands in her lap and stared down at them. "I'm sorry. I sort of freaked out."

"About us?"

"Yes. No. I mean, mostly about me. I've had this thing about setting a good example for Jenna." She glanced up at him. "She might have mentioned it?"

He covered her hands with one of his, and she didn't push him away. "She did."

"Why didn't you tell me?"

"I'm pretty sure she shared that in confidence and I didn't want to risk losing her trust. For all I knew, she was testing me."

Kristi smiled at that. "It's what teenagers do. And it turns out they're a lot smarter than we...I...give them credit for."

She told him about the conversation she'd had with Jenna that morning and while she did, he thought of ways he might thank the girl. She had hinted that her friends would think a pool party would be the coolest thing ever. *Well, Jenna. Prepare to be cool.*

"So to summarize," he said, "you think you need to set a good example, and she thinks you don't."

"Pretty much."

"Any chance you'll agree with her?"

She unfolded her hands and intertwined her fingers with his. A hopeful sign…he hoped.

"I want to, I'd like to, but…"

All he could do was hold his breath and wait.

"I need to take this slowly. The other night…" Her color deepened. "That was not slow."

She was right. If she'd said no, that it was too soon to take their relationship into the bedroom, it might have killed him but he would have stopped.

"I hope you didn't feel pressured."

"No! No, not at all. But we both have kids to think about, and even though Jenna says I don't need to worry about her, I do. You and I just met, and if she knew we were already sleeping together… Well, that's not the message I want to send."

She was right about this, too, and he was reminded of his mother's words of wisdom. *Blended families are a big adjustment. They take work, and patience.* It was too soon to talk about them being a family, but he needed to put the rest of her advice into practice.

"Listen, the last thing I want to do is send the wrong message to Jenna, or Molly and Martha. What if we slow things down, give them a chance to get on board with this? No more sleepovers until they get used to us being a couple."

"You'd be willing to do that?"

"For them, yes." *For you, anything.* He wanted to be in her and Jenna's lives, and he needed them in his and the twins'. He'd do whatever it took.

To demonstrate just slow it could be, he slid his hands

up her arms and gently eased her in for a kiss, just a light touch of his lips to hers. As he pulled back, her eyelids fluttered open and her smile told him everything he needed to know. Well, almost everything. "I still have one question."

"What's that?"

"What's in the bag you brought with you?"

Her smile widened. "A housewarming present. Come on, I'll show you."

She stood and picked up the blue shopping bag, extending her other hand to him. He took it and let her lead him to the breakfast bar. She set the bag on the counter and after they'd each taken a stool, she pulled out a rectangular box wrapped in plain brown paper. "I made this for your office. I hope you like it."

He tore the paper away and stared at the framed photobooth strips until the lump in his throat subsided enough for him to speak. "I... Wow... I don't know what to say."

"If you don't like it—"

"No, I love it, thank you."

"I'm glad. I made two more for the girls, and one that you might want to have in your office at the university."

He liked that she would create something so personal. To him, it felt the opposite of taking things slowly, and he loved that. He loved her. And he thanked her the best way he could, with a kiss that let her know there was nothing wrong with speeding things up once in a while.

Chapter Fifteen

The summer had flown by and it had been pretty close to perfect in Kristi's opinion. Nate had decided not to sell his home after all, and she and Jenna had spent many happy hours there with him and the twins. Jenna was teaching Molly and Martha how to swim. Kristi was rediscovering the joy of having young children in her life again, and her biological clock was ticking a little less loudly. She'd learned the best example to set for Jenna was being in a healthy, committed relationship. And Nate, the same great dad he'd always been, was more confident and even more patient than ever. Nate had found the nerve to have that talk with his mother-in-law, so Kristi worked up the courage to have the talk with her daughter.

Today they were at the mall, all five of them, shopping for school clothes. Kristi was surprised that Jenna had agreed to tag along, and even more surprised that her daughter was cheerfully accompanying them from store to store, and not begging to go off on her own. Whatever the reason, Kristi didn't intend to question her behavior. She was too happy, strolling hand in hand with Nate, listening to Jenna's running commentary on outfits worn by other shoppers and keeping a close watch on Molly and Martha. This felt like a real family, as real as it got.

"Daddy, there's the photo booth," Martha said.

Molly hopped up and down. "Let's take our pictures."

Nate looked down at her. "You don't mind?"

Kristi smiled up at him. "You know I don't. Go ahead. Jenna and I will wait here for you."

Nate handed coins to the girls, who fed them into the slot, then he followed them into the booth and pulled the curtain closed. A couple of minutes later they appeared, the girls giggling over the new strip. Nate smiled and waved her over.

Kristi shook her head. She hated being photographed.

"Oh, Mom," Jenna prodded her. "Go have your picture taken. It'll be cute."

"Cute? Who are you, and what have you done with my daughter."

Jenna gave her a playful shove toward Nate. "Go. I'll watch the kidlets."

He took her hand, and while she smoothed her hair, he did that thing with his thumb on her palm that always made her shiver.

"You look beautiful." His credit card went into the slot, then he swept the curtain aside for her. "After you."

Kristi ducked inside and sat down. "I've never done this before."

"Neither have I." He settled in next to her, his thigh pressed firmly against hers.

What was that supposed to mean? He and the girls had done this dozens of times.

"This light lets you know when the next photo will be taken."

"What am I supposed to do?"

"Be yourself. Ready?"

The light blinked.

"I love you, Kristi."

That made her laugh. "I love you, too."

The light blinked a second time.

"Will you marry me?" Nate was holding a ring.

He was proposing? He was proposing! "Yes, I'll marry you."

He slid the ring onto her finger.

She blinked. So did the light. It was the most beautiful ring she'd ever seen.

And then he kissed her and she closed her eyes and saw something that looked a lot like fireworks.

"Our pictures are ready," he said a moment later.

Her hands were shaking, so he held up the strip so she could see it.

In the first frame, they were gazing into each other's eyes and wearing the goofiest smiles imaginable. In the second she was staring wide-eyed at the ring. In the third photo the ring was on her finger, and in the fourth his lips were on hers.

This was the most romantic thing that had ever happened to her, and now she was engaged—engaged!—and she still hadn't really looked at her ring. She held up her hand and got a little teary. A princess-cut diamond solitaire in a stunning art deco setting.

"Nate, it's beautiful. It looks…old."

"It is. Jenna helped me pick it out."

"She knows?"

"I needed to be sure she was okay with it."

The curtain whipped open and Jenna stuck her head in. "What's taking so long?"

"She said yes."

Jenna launched herself into the booth and the twins followed, and then everyone was laughing and talking at the same time.

"Do you like the ring?" Jenna asked.

"I love it."

"I knew you would. I helped pick it out."

Kristi looked from her daughter to her fiancé—she had a fiancé!—and her heart suddenly felt too big for her chest.

"Nate said I can have an iPhone," Jenna announced.

"An engagement present," he said. "Figured it was the least I could do for the help with the ring."

"And he's going to let me drive the Volkswagen!"

His arm tightened around Kristi's shoulder. "After you get your license," he said. "And if your mom says it's okay."

"You're going to spoil her." But Kristi knew he wouldn't. He was Jenna's dad now, every bit as much as he was Molly's and Martha's. Over the tops of three blond heads, she looked at Nate and she knew she had it all…the man, the family and the home of her dreams.

* * * * *

REQUEST YOUR FREE BOOKS!

2 FREE NOVELS PLUS 2 *FREE GIFTS!*

❧ Harlequin®

American ★ *Romance*®

LOVE, HOME & HAPPINESS

YES! Please send me 2 FREE Harlequin® American Romance® novels and my 2 FREE gifts (gifts are worth about $10). After receiving them, if I don't wish to receive any more books, I can return the shipping statement marked "cancel." If I don't cancel, I will receive 4 brand-new novels every month and be billed just $4.49 per book in the U.S. or $5.24 per book in Canada. That's a saving of at least 14% off the cover price! It's quite a bargain! Shipping and handling is just 50¢ per book in the U.S. and 75¢ per book in Canada.* I understand that accepting the 2 free books and gifts places me under no obligation to buy anything. I can always return a shipment and cancel at any time. Even if I never buy another book, the two free books and gifts are mine to keep forever.

154/354 HDN FEP2

Name	(PLEASE PRINT)	
Address		Apt. #
City	State/Prov.	Zip/Postal Code

Signature (if under 18, a parent or guardian must sign)

Mail to the **Reader Service:**
IN U.S.A.: P.O. Box 1867, Buffalo, NY 14240-1867
IN CANADA: P.O. Box 609, Fort Erie, Ontario L2A 5X3

Not valid for current subscribers to Harlequin American Romance books.

Want to try two free books from another line?
Call 1-800-873-8635 or visit www.ReaderService.com.

* Terms and prices subject to change without notice. Prices do not include applicable taxes. Sales tax applicable in N.Y. Canadian residents will be charged applicable taxes. Offer not valid in Quebec. This offer is limited to one order per household. All orders subject to credit approval. Credit or debit balances in a customer's account(s) may be offset by any other outstanding balance owed by or to the customer. Please allow 4 to 6 weeks for delivery. Offer available while quantities last.

Your Privacy—The Reader Service is committed to protecting your privacy. Our Privacy Policy is available online at www.ReaderService.com or upon request from the Reader Service.

We make a portion of our mailing list available to reputable third parties that offer products we believe may interest you. If you prefer that we not exchange your name with third parties, or if you wish to clarify or modify your communication preferences, please visit us at www.ReaderService.com/consumerchoice or write to us at Reader Service Preference Service, P.O. Box 9062, Buffalo, NY 14269. Include your complete name and address.

HARI1B

Turn the page for a preview of
THE OTHER SIDE OF US
by
Sarah Mayberry,
coming January 2013
from Harlequin® Superromance®.

PLUS, exciting changes are in the works!
Enjoy the same great stories in a longer format
and new look—beginning January 2013!

Coming January 2013

THE OTHER SIDE OF US
A brand-new novel
from Harlequin® Superromance® author
Sarah Mayberry

*In recovery from a serious accident, Mackenzie Williams
is beating all the doctors' predictions. But she needs
single-minded focus. She* doesn't *need the distraction
of neighbors—especially good-looking ones
like Oliver Garrett!*

MACKENZIE BREATHED DEEPLY to recover from the workout. She'd pushed herself too far but she wanted to accelerate her rehabilitation. Still, she needed to lie down to combat the nausea and shaking muscles.

There was a knock on the front door. Who on earth would be visiting her on a Thursday morning? Probably a cold-calling salesperson.

She answered, but her pithy rejection died before she'd formed the first words.

The man on her doorstep was definitely not a cold caller. Nothing about this man was cold, from the auburn of his wavy hair to his brown eyes to his sensual mouth. Nothing cold about those broad shoulders, flat belly and lean hips, either.

"Hey," he said in a shiver-inducing baritone. "I'm Oliver Garrett. I moved in next door." His smile was so warm and vibrant it was almost offensive.

"Mackenzie Williams." Oh, no. Her legs were starting to

HSREXP1212HH

tremble, indicating they wouldn't hold up long. Any second now she would embarrass herself in front of this complete and very good-looking stranger.

"It's been years since I was down here." He seemed to settle in for a chat. "It doesn't look as though—"

"I have to go." Her stomach rolled as she shut the door. The last thing she registered was the look of shock on Oliver's face at her abrupt dismissal.

And somehow she knew their neighborly relations would be a lot cooler now.

*Will Mackenzie be able to make it up to Oliver
for her rude introduction?
Find out in THE OTHER SIDE OF US
by Sarah Mayberry, available January 2013 from
Harlequin® Superromance®. PLUS, exciting changes are
in the works! Enjoy the same great stories in a longer
format and new look—beginning January 2013!*